CHRISTIANA

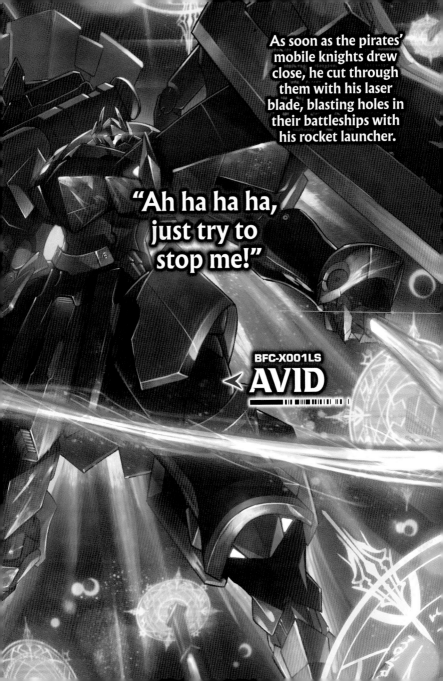

As soon as the pirates' mobile knights drew close, he cut through them with his laser blade, blasting holes in their battleships with his rocket launcher.

"Ah ha ha ha, just try to stop me!"

BFC-X001LS
AVID

CONTENTS

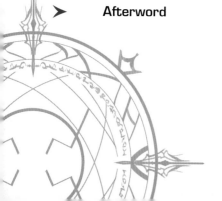

I'M THE EVIL LORD OF AN INTERGALACTIC EMPIRE

NOVEL

WRITTEN BY

YOMU MISHIMA

ILLUSTRATED BY

NADARE TAKAMINE

Airship

Seven Seas Entertainment

ORE WA SEIKAN KOKKA NO AKUTOKU RYOUSHU! Vol. 1
©2020 Yomu Mishima
First published in Japan in 2020 by OVERLAP Inc., Ltd., Tokyo.
English translation rights arranged with OVERLAP Inc., Ltd., Tokyo.

Seven Seas press and purchase enquiries can be sent to
Marketing Manager Lianne Sentar at press@gomanga.com.
Information regarding the distribution and purchase of
digital editions is available from Digital Manager CK Russell
at digital@gomanga.com.

Follow Seven Seas Entertainment online at
sevenseasentertainment.com.

TRANSLATION: Amy Osteraas
ADAPTATION: Jeffrey Thomas
COVER DESIGN: Hanase Qi
INTERIOR LAYOUT & DESIGN: Clay Gardner
PROOFREADER: Meg van Huygen
LIGHT NOVEL EDITOR: T. Anne
PREPRESS TECHNICIAN: Rhiannon Rasmussen-Silverstein
PRODUCTION MANAGER: Lissa Pattillo
MANAGING EDITOR: Julie Davis
ASSOCIATE PUBLISHER: Adam Arnold
PUBLISHER: Jason DeAngelis

ISBN: 978-1-64827-657-6
Printed in Canada
First Printing: November 2021
10 9 8 7 6 5 4 3 2 1

Prologue

FROM THE COCKPIT MONITOR, I looked out into space. Lights sparkled all around me, and explosions too—like something straight out of science fiction. Countless tiny streaks of light flashed in the distance, some resulting in small explosions. Inside each and every one of those explosions, hundreds or perhaps thousands of lives were snuffed out.

Space battles take the lives of a vast number of people. During one such battle, where tens or hundreds of thousands of people might perish, I raised my voice and laughed aloud.

"What's wrong? Is that all you've got?"

The weapon I piloted was a humanoid vehicle—a mobile knight. As weapons, these fourteen-meter behemoths presented a number of flaws. Why did they have to be humanoid in form, instead of something like fighter jets? This fantasy world seemed unconcerned with such rational questions, however.

My mobile knight was black and titanic. While most other units were around eighteen meters tall, this one was on the larger side at twenty-four meters. In my mammoth machine, I grabbed smaller units around me with my manipulators, as its dexterous hands were called, and crushed my enemies' machines along with the pilots inside them.

"Please, spare me!"

An enemy pilot begged for his life, but I just smirked coldly and said, "Die."

There wasn't a speck of pity in my voice. I felt no guilt killing my enemies, only joy. Trampling another person and taking their most precious possession from them, their life...that was a privilege only the strong possessed.

"Weak. Too weak. Isn't there anyone *strong*?"

I laughed as I piloted my craft, mowing down all the enemies that approached me. I aimed for their cockpits and the pilots within. I mercilessly thrust the laser sword gripped in my mobile knight's hand into an enemy cockpit, then kicked the unit away, ripping the blade back out.

"You weaklings are nothing but prey! At least *try* to entertain me!"

All this horror was the work of a boy who appeared to be in his early teens. In my previous life, I would have objected to such inhuman acts, but now I knew better. It's the bad people who have all the advantages. That was why I'd vowed to be a villain in my next life. No—a supervillain!

If someone were to describe my current position, they would call me an "evil lord." In this strange, fantastical land, humanity had advanced far enough for intergalactic travel, yet it still had a completely outdated aristocratic form of government. In this world, I was a count. I ruled over a planet of my own, terrorizing my subjects. If this were a story, I'd be the villain for the protagonist to defeat. But in reality...

"Are you done? Come on, come at me! I haven't had enough. Give me more!"

I chased after the enemies fleeing from my machine and took them down without mercy, a textbook villain. This world had no heroes. I could torment the weak all I liked and no one would stop me. In this place, might made right. That was the conclusion I had reached at the moment of my death in my previous life.

"Ahh, this is so much fun. Crushing weaklings is the *best*. It just confirms how strong I am."

In this world, people warred with giant humanoid weapons and spaceships. Reincarnated into such a world, I intended to use the immense power I'd been given to live a life of tyranny.

It all started on that day—the last day of my previous life, when I was deceived and died in the pit of despair. The harsh memories revived in my mind, memories of a man who'd led a foolish life, not even realizing that he was being destroyed. Yes, in my previous life, that fool was me.

Why do I have to go through things like this?

I clutched at my chest in my shoddy, one-room apartment. It had been bothering me for a while now, but recently the pain had gotten a lot worse. I would have gone to the hospital, but I didn't have the money.

My hand pawed helplessly at my chest, too weak to exert any force. The bruised arm reaching into my unwashed T-shirt was thinner than it used to be. I coughed up blood, staining the filthy futon I lay on.

"Why...is this...happening to me?"

I was in physical pain, but the mental anguish and the frustration I felt were no less painful. As they say, my life was flashing before my eyes. I was by no means a saint, but I had tried to live an honest life. I'd never committed a crime, and I'd lived as best I could according to the standards of virtue set by society.

I'd gotten a job like I was supposed to, gotten married as expected, had a kid, and bought a house. Yet I was now shouldering debt and working multiple part-time jobs. I paid child support every month, yet I'd never once seen my daughter since the divorce. According to my ex-wife, our daughter was finally starting to get along with her new husband, which was why she kept denying me visitation.

Meanwhile, the company I used to work for had fired me for having an affair and embezzling, neither of which I had done, and I'd had to get multiple part-time gigs just to survive. I'd never had an affair, and I'd never embezzled any money, but no matter how much I denied both claims, everyone around me treated me as though I were guilty. No one believed a word I said.

I'd never forget the despair I felt at the time. I was treated with such scorn by those around me that I had to wonder now if I really *was* to blame for it all. That was how much their words affected me.

And now, I'd hit rock bottom. I had so much debt that I would never be able to repay it, and I was living in poverty in a tiny room with hardly any belongings. Nearly every day, some thug or another came demanding I repay my debts, but I didn't even remember borrowing any money. Still, for some reason, there were debts in my name that I was obligated to repay. Now that I thought about it, it was probably my ex-wife's doing, but I didn't have the funds or the energy to talk to a lawyer about it.

At some point in the last few years, without realizing it, I'd started to waste away. I looked a lot older than I actually was. Every time I glanced in the mirror, I seemed to be on the verge of death.

"What did I do? Just where...where did I go wrong?"

Every time I coughed, I spat up more and more blood. *It looks like this is the end.* Overwhelmed with all this frustration, I was just relieved that it would finally be over.

That was when it happened.

A man in a striped tailcoat appeared beside my futon. He stood on my dirty tatami floor in his shoes, a traveling bag in one hand.

"Good evening. And what a lovely evening it is."

I shifted my gaze, and in my hazy vision, I saw a man with a top hat in one hand greeting me. His eyes were hidden in shadow, so all I could see of his face was his mouth. He was tall and thin, looking down at me from above.

Something about him didn't seem real. The brim of his hat and the ends of his tailcoat moved strangely, and though he wasn't on fire, he was emitting a peculiar smoke. I doubted he was of this world.

"What are you, some sort of ferryman?" I asked, my voice hoarse and weak. It hurt my chest just to talk. I didn't have the energy to scramble away in fright, nor did I plan on it. All I felt was a sense of resignation and the hope that I would finally be free from my suffering.

Then I remembered something. Many years ago, I'd heard that when you died, an old pet from your past would come to guide you away. I'd had a dog long ago, but it hadn't come to meet me. *Guess that was just made up—or I wasn't a good owner.* If I had one regret, it was that my dog hadn't been the one to come get me.

The man knelt down beside me, drawing closer, but I still couldn't see his face above his mouth. The corners of his lips lifted into a crescent-moon smile, as though he were laughing at me.

"True, I am a ferryman in a sense, though I'm not taking you where you think I am. The truth is, I'm here to send you to a different world. Therefore, you can just call me your Guide."

"A d—ff—wor—!" I started coughing, and the man snapped his fingers.

I was shocked to find that the view in front of me had completely changed. I saw a man in an expensive suit having dinner with my ex-wife in a fancy restaurant. The meal set before them looked delicious, as did the alcohol they were drinking. I hadn't had anything like that in years.

That wasn't what shocked me, though. How could I be witnessing this scene that floated before my eyes? I wondered if I was dreaming, but the pain in my chest felt as real as ever. And it wasn't just physical pain: there was pain in my heart as well. I also heard the conspiratorial conversation the two were having.

"You're a real piece of work, aren't you? You foist all that debt onto your ex-husband, and you make him pay child support too. It's not even his kid."

Clearly it was me they were discussing, but I couldn't believe what they were saying. No, I didn't *want* to believe it.

"It's fine. Legally, it's his kid, and child support is a parent's duty, isn't it?"

I struggled to wrap my head around it. What was my ex-wife saying? In the past, she had been kind, even naive, yet here she was talking about deceiving me with a nasty smile on her face, like a completely different person. *Like* a different person, but unmistakably my ex-wife.

"Women instinctively seek out men with superior genes to have children with. I didn't need a kid with a man like him; I just needed him to make me some money. Actually,

he should be grateful since I allowed him to marry me. He was only ever worth that much."

The man seated across from her seemed exasperated by her words, but his expression also suggested he was enjoying it.

"Women are scary."

"You're the one who made me this way, aren't you?"

Watching them only made my chest hurt more. Rage bubbled up inside me at this scene and at the Guide who'd revealed it to me.

"Oh, don't be angry. I only showed you this because I wanted you to know the truth. It makes sense, doesn't it? It's not an illusion—this is something that's occurring right now."

When I thought about it, it did start to make sense. Until now, I had closed my eyes to it under the impression that I was merely overthinking things.

"You have a truly good heart, enduring a life like this and still working hard to repay her debt and pay child support. Yet all this time, it was nothing but lies! Can they really get away with such evil? In response to these injustices, I've prepared a little present for you."

The man merrily removed some pamphlets resembling travel brochures from his leather bag.

"You've been very unfortunate in this life. In your next

life, wouldn't you like to be happy? What do you think? How would you like to be reborn in a different world?"

A different world? I could barely process what he was saying, I was so full of rage and frustration toward my ex-wife. My chest throbbed again, and I spat up more blood. I realized something else then too.

"W-was the embezzling also—" I asked, regarding my former job, and the Guide nodded.

"Yes, that's right. That was your boss, who framed you for his crime. You did nothing wrong."

I get it now. What a fool I've been. I was deceived over and over again.

"You've worked so hard that your body gave out on you, and here they are, enjoying a decadent meal together. It's just horrible, isn't it?"

I gripped my futon. What had been the meaning of my life? Why was it ending this way?

"Revenge... Let me take revenge. I can't...let them get away with it. I want revenge...on all of them."

My tears of frustration felt endless. Even they were bloody now. Why was this my fate? What had I done to deserve it? I cried at the state of my body, which could barely move anymore. I would never be able to take revenge like this.

For a moment, the Guide's smile grew even wider, but

it swiftly vanished. It didn't seem as though he would grant my wish.

"Unfortunately, your life is at its end. All I can give you is the gift of a happy second life. This one has been cruel to you, but your next life awaits. I'm afraid you'll have to give up on revenge."

"N-no!" I squeezed out, barely able to utter the word.

At this point, no matter how much I suffered, I just wanted to make them suffer too. I would do anything for that—anything!

Yet the Guide just shook his head. "All you can choose is what sort of world you'd like to live in next. Go and be reincarnated in the world you desire. A happy life is waiting for you this time."

I sobbed in vexation.

The Guide held out his pamphlets like a magician asking me to choose a card. One of the worlds he offered was a place of swords and magic, another a place just like Earth but with the existence of superpowers. In yet another, the landmasses floated in the air with the clouds. None of them really spoke to me except for one with a humanoid machine and a space battleship on its cover. I reached out to this pamphlet, my consciousness hazy. When my bloody fingers touched the brochure, the Guide began his explanation.

"Ah, you're interested in this world? I recommend it. It's a fantastical place with both advanced science and magic, after all, not to mention an intergalactic empire. It's really quite fun. People live long lives there as well, so you can look forward to living much longer than you did here."

I'd chosen without thinking all that much, except how crazy it all sounded.

What had I even lived an honest life for? For *this*? To be deceived, laughed at—without even being able to take revenge for it?

It's so unfair! If this is what happens when you're good, then I should have enjoyed my life more. I should have worried more about my own happiness without sparing a thought for other people. Good karma isn't worth shit. It's all a lie. And if that's the case, then I wanna live for myself.

I'll live for myself as a villain who tramples other people underfoot.

"Hmm, in this world...if you want power, you'd have to be nobility. These people are culturally advanced, but for some reason, the feudal system made a big comeback at some point. It's quite interesting." The Guide continued his explanation as he watched me writhe in pain. "I'll make it so you're born into a noble house. You'll start your next life as an aristocrat with a silver spoon in your mouth, as they say."

I wanted to smile at his words, but I didn't have the luxury. I was in so much pain now that I couldn't even respond. My soul, however, would live on past this body, and I would never forget this day. *Living an honest life is idiotic. If I'm going to be born an aristocrat, then I'll be able to do whatever I want in my next life. I'll rule with an iron fist and be as evil as I please.*

The Guide was doing his part, setting things up for me. "A count sounds good. That would put you in charge of a planet."

That sounds great. A pretty important position. I'll be an evil mage—no, I'll be ruling over a planet, so an evil lord? Anyway, I'm gonna enjoy myself.

"So you've made your peace? I trust you'll have a nice life next time, then..."

Yeah. I think I will. I'll make my next life a good one. My life as an evil lord.

At that point, my consciousness faded into darkness.

The Guide looked down at the man, who had died with a smile on his face. He twisted around, grinning with insane glee.

"An unhappy life? Gimme a break! People as unhappy

as you are a dime a dozen in this world! You think you had it bad? You're deluded!"

With a snap of his fingers, the image of the man's ex-wife and her lover was projected into the air once again. Cackling obscenely, he observed the pair.

"You two sure came in handy, didn't you? Well, I've enjoyed myself enough. Let's wrap this up."

This man who called himself a Guide was decidedly not the type to wish for another's happiness. Just the opposite, in fact. He looked down at the dead man in front of him and laughed, pointing his finger.

"Who do you think made you unhappy in the first place? It was me! I just wanted to see how far I could make a good person fall. I got a lot more fun out of it than I thought I would, though, so I came up with a continuation to make it last."

This Guide was basically a creature composed of malice who loved unhappiness and lived on it as sustenance. Negative emotions, especially from people *he* made miserable, were his greatest nourishment. He had done it countless times; the man lying before him was just one such victim.

"Now then, before the main course, I should polish off the *hors d'oeuvres*."

He reached out and touched the image, and black

smoke poured out of him. It coiled around the pair in the projected image, but they didn't notice. As they discussed the dead man, their cheerful conversation started to change.

The man's smile faded, his expression turning grave. He said to the woman, *"Well, we've both had our fun, haven't we? I think it's about time to end things."*

"Huh?"

The Guide chuckled, relishing this turn of events. "Now, show me how far *you* will fall."

Dumbfounded, the woman dropped the knife she'd been holding. *"Wh-what are you saying?"*

"I'm saying our little play-relationship is over. It's run its course, right?"

She looked lost, bewildered. *"Are you joking? If you're serious, then you know you're going down. You think I don't know all the things you've done?"*

The man was cool in the face of her threats. *"If you want to put up a fight, then by all means, do it, but don't forget that the lawyer who helped you with your divorce is a friend of mine. If you make a scene, you'll be the one who ends up in hot water. I'll expose you for setting up your ex-husband and helping his boss embezzle from his company."*

"Wh-what about your daughter? You're just going to abandon your own child?"

"Legally, it's his kid, right? Plus, he's paying child support, isn't he? I'm sure you'll do fine."

When she realized he was being serious, the ex-wife could only tremble. She barely managed to squeeze out, *"You said you loved me."*

"And I did, but I've lost interest—that's all there is to it. If we both enjoyed it while it lasted, that's fine, right? Just find your next love."

"I can't do that!"

The ex-wife clung to the man, but he peeled her hands off him and made to leave the restaurant. *"Don't touch me. I'm not interested in you anymore."*

"Wait, please, listen to me! I'll do anything! Don't leave me!"

The ex-wife pleaded desperately, but the man simply looked at her with eyes like ice. They were nothing like the couple who'd been happily chatting a few minutes earlier.

"What are you, stupid? You really thought I was gonna marry a cheater like you? Use your head, why don't you? If your ex-husband fell in love with you, then he had terrible taste."

If those words were true, then this man had never loved the ex-wife from the beginning. When he'd said he loved her, he'd lied. Realizing that, she couldn't even bring herself to speak anymore.

Clapping gleefully, the Guide said, "Fantastic! What will she do next?"

The ex-wife's despair flowed into him. He gobbled up her rage and sadness—all her negative emotions. They filled the Guide's heart, satiating him.

With clenched fists, the woman hung her head. *"I left my husband for you."*

"Your ex-*husband. And you enjoyed driving him into a corner, didn't you? Don't pretend you're the victim here. You were the one who left him."*

"You said it!" The Guide laughed in agreement, then read the ex-wife's thoughts. "Oh my, she's reconsidering him now, even though he's already dead. Women sure are tough. It's too bad; the man who loved you is dead, and his last desire was to have revenge on you!"

The Guide cackled, banishing the scene in order to enjoy the next step of his plans. "I look forward to seeing if you try to go back to your husband, or if you try to find a new man. Unfortunately, happiness will never come to you!"

He'd made sure either option would only lead to more unhappiness. That was what it meant when the Guide stepped into one's life.

"Now then, I have to guide his soul...to a world where lives are cheaply consumed. A happy world. For me, that is!"

The Guide couldn't stop smiling, thinking about the world he was about to enter.

"By the time he realizes it, it'll be too late. This is going to be so much fun. 'It wasn't supposed to be like this!' he'll cry. He'll be filled with resentment, anger, sadness... and it'll all be directed at me! He'll hate me, and his hate will only nourish me!"

The Guide, who loved nothing more than the negative emotions of humans, spread his arms wide. He simply couldn't contain his mirth when he imagined the feelings his scheme would soon produce.

"Whether he becomes a villain and sows despair in that other world or becomes unhappy himself and over-flows with hatred for me, I win! Now, it's time for my fun to begin!"

No matter how things went, he was certain to enjoy himself. The Guide's anticipation reached the point of ecstasy.

"Oh, it's almost time. I'll return here after I finish guid-ing his soul. These fools...they all rejoice when they hear they'll be reincarnated. These are truly fantastic times. All it takes is a few sweet lies and they fall for it."

He picked up his bag excitedly and, with a snap of his fingers, summoned a lavishly decorated wooden door, which looked completely out of place in the shabby apartment. This was his means of traversing the many realities. The Guide turned the knob and opened the door, revealing a swirling mass of black and purple. He stood there for a moment, lifting a hand to his chin in thought.

In a corner of the room, a small light seemed to observe the Guide. The vague light watched him in secret, but it gradually grew larger and took on a more defined shape. Its outline was blurred, but it appeared to be a dog. After casting a forlorn look at the deceased man, the figure of light glared at the Guide, though it went unnoticed.

"I don't know how I should make the most of this. Let's see, first I'll have to decide where to reincarnate him. It's fun enough putting him in a happy family and making him suffer afterward, and I did just do that...but maybe better to have him work his way up and then knock him back down? I wouldn't want him thanking me for the opportunity before the fall, though."

The Guide clapped his hands together. "Well, I'll play it by ear for now, though at the end, I think torture and a public execution would be good. I'm looking forward to seeing him curse me and die in despair. Ah! I can hardly wait." The Guide embraced himself and squirmed with mad glee.

"Your next life should be longer than this one. Longer and more painful as well! I do hope you'll struggle throughout for the sake of my happiness!" Making up his mind, the Guide headed through the door looking rather refreshed. However, unbeknownst to him, the little dog made of light leapt through the door with him.

When the door to the other world closed, it vanished from the room, whose only occupant now was the man's lifeless body.

I'M THE **EVIL LORD** OF AN
**INTERGALACTIC
EMPIRE**

1 Liam

IT SEEMS THE GUIDE was telling the truth. Here I am in my second life, after all.

My new name was Liam Sera Banfield. When I looked in the mirror, I saw a boy with black hair and amethyst eyes. This reflection waved back at me when I waved, so I was certain it was me.

I was five years old, playing in a child's room, when I became conscious of my past life. There were numerous toys on the floor around me, but what immediately caught my eye was the size of the room.

"Pretty big." Even taking my vantage point into account, the room was large. It was a child's playroom, but it could probably have fit a small house inside it.

I appeared to be pretty well-off. The Guide had told me I'd be born into a noble's house, someone with authority, and he must have kept his word. My vague memories of my current life confirmed that. This was the family of Count Banfield, and I was his heir. The count ruled a planet in the Intergalactic Algrand Empire of the Albareto Dynasty. In the future, *I* would rule this planet. In the scale of the entire Empire, my station wasn't too impressive, but I liked the sound of "ruler of a planet." There would be no one on my entire planet who could defy me.

"As promised." I smirked.

I didn't know why the Guide had chosen me for reincarnation, but I would probably betray his expectations. If he was expecting me to do good in this world, then I was going to have to disappoint him. After all, I'd learned in my previous life that doing good was worthless. I planned on becoming a striking example of an evil lord. Of course, that presented me with my first problem.

"What does an evil lord or, like, a bad noble even do?" In fiction, they would oppress their people, so should I do the same? When I thought of "evil," what came to mind was booze, women, and gambling. *Does that sound right?*

"Should I just be a glutton?" My image of an evil lord was rather vague. *Should I increase taxes and accept bribes, like a crooked politician? Well, I'm sure that just doing as I please is fine.*

"This is getting pretty exciting, hm?"

Something fluttered down to land on my head. I picked it up and saw that it was a letter. When I opened the neatly sealed envelope, I found a message from the Guide inside.

"He sent me a letter? Why not just show himself again?"

I found the answer to my question within its contents. It started with congratulations for my successful rein-carnation. Then it told me the Guide was busy, so he wouldn't be able to watch over me for some time, but that he would make sure I got the assistance I needed. Apparently, someone else would provide help in his place.

"Help? In this place? From whom?" I was alone in the room, with no one else nearby.

While I cocked my head, curious, the door opened. A man and woman stepped into the room, attended by a group of people behind them. Their names surfaced in my mind; my memories told me that these were my current parents.

My father was Cliff Sera Banfield, my mother Darcie Sera Banfield. The pair walked over to me with smiles on their faces and handed me something that looked like a glass tablet. I saw some sort of document, apparently a contract, on the green-tinted surface. The writing was unfamiliar to me, but I seemed able to read some of it nonetheless. It appeared to indicate that my father's peerage and domain were being transferred to me.

They're just giving everything to a little kid? I was a bit confused by the sudden development.

"Father, what's this?" I wasn't sure how to handle this news and, more than anything else, these new parents of mine were nothing more than a bother to me, really. They didn't show up all that much in the vague memories I retained. *What's going on here?*

I looked up at the man I had awkwardly addressed, and he patiently explained things to me. After he'd spoken, though, I was even more confused.

"Happy fifth birthday, Liam. My present for you is everything that House Banfield owns."

Everything the Banfield family owns as a birthday present? You're giving your peerage, your domain, and all the responsibilities that come with them to a five-year-old child for his birthday? Is this guy serious?

So I thought, but then I recalled the letter I'd just read. It had vanished from my hands at some point, but I wondered if this was what the Guide had meant by "help." Such a wild turn of events might be possible for a supernatural being like him.

Next, my mother Darcie happily held out a catalog to

me. "And this is my present. I'll buy you a robotic maid to take care of you. Pick whichever one you like."

On the cover of the catalog was a robot that had been created to look like a maid. Actually, it looked just like a human, so I figured it was an android.

When I opened the catalog, it projected images and videos around me that I could view from all angles. It felt very futuristic, which was intriguing, but I wasn't really sure what came next.

"Wh-what do I do with this?"

Darcie kindly explained how to use the catalog. "You can use this to customize your maid. It's easy. Just choose which parts you want, like this. See? Go ahead, make a nice, cute one."

Apparently, you ordered robots like you were creating a character in a game. You chose not just their appearance but also the internal parts and materials that determined their functionality. It was pretty interesting.

I chose all the high-performance parts, which made a number at the bottom—I assumed that was the price— shoot up with each selection. It was already three digits higher than it had been originally, but I wasn't the one paying for it, so I decided to make the maid ridiculously high-spec.

For its looks, how about an Eastern beauty? Her hair

would be long and black, tied back in a ponytail, bangs a little longer on the right. I made sure to give her a good figure too.

As I went through, choosing various attributes, my hands stopped at a certain selection. Now this was surprising. Cliff teased me for hesitating, which annoyed me, but he didn't seem to understand why I'd stopped. He eyed the 3D projection of the model I'd constructed so far.

"He sure is my son. He's got great taste."

"Children do love breasts, don't they?"

I ignored the two of them and slowly made the selection that I'd been hesitating over. It added...an adult aspect to the robot. My parents just smiled as they watched their child order a robot that was fully functional for sex. *What a bizarre situation this is.*

The complex expression on the face of the aged but stately butler standing behind them, Brian Beaumont, left quite an impression on me. He looked at once saddened and confused. *My parents really are weirdos, right?*

Anyway, something else had occurred to me at this point. Was the "helper" that the Guide had referred to actually this maid robot that I was ordering?

So the first thing he does is get rid of these annoying parents of mine and give me the ideal woman to stand at my side and act as his agent? I am thoroughly impressed by his consideration. These parents would likely only bother me, so it'll be easier if they're just not around. Plus...I can't trust a real woman. A maid robot is truly a thoughtful gift for me. After all, I don't have to worry about betrayal from a robot.

It said so right on the catalog, under the slogan "A maid just for you!" at the top: "Maid robots will never betray their masters." If I had a faithful, capable retainer whom I needn't worry about betraying me, that would give me some real peace of mind. Thus, I kept ignoring the price and tacking on as many optional features as I could.

After the final confirmation of her specs was a screen to pick out the maid's uniform. I selected a classical outfit, since a miniskirt would really be too much. I hesitated a bit over whether I wanted the length to be above or below her knees, but in the end, I decided on just above her ankles.

"My, how cute." Happily looking over the completed model, Darcie was another strange sight. *Your son just bought a maid designed completely to his adult tastes and fully functional for sex. What exactly about that makes you so happy?*

"We can leave Liam in the care of this robot now, can't we?" she asked.

"Yep. Nothin' to worry about now," Cliff agreed.

Suspicious of my parents' attitude, I asked them, "Are you going somewhere?"

Cliff raised his chin and proudly declared, "We've bought a mansion on the Imperial Home Planet, the capital. We'll be moving there, and you'll stay here and protect your domain as its lord. You just have to sign this document first."

I looked down at the electronic document that transferred my father's title and land to me. All the servants around us looked rather confused, so this must have been an unusual occurrence. *I mean, it's gotta be, right? This guy's giving everything he owns to a five-year-old. "Unusual" doesn't even cover it.*

Once I'd signed the document, Darcie handed me another one. "Here you go, Liam. Sign this one too." This document guaranteed that I sent my parents living on the Capital Planet a sort of yearly allowance.

They're giving everything to me and going to live in the capital, eh? These two are really some sorry excuses for parents. Unbeknownst to them, their darling son is a reincarnation, a middle-aged dude on the inside. It's kind of hilarious.

It was actually pitiful that this man and woman would have their status and everything they owned taken away by basically a complete stranger. I still didn't see them as my real parents, but I felt bad enough for them that I supposed I would send them some money every year.

"Okay!" I chirped. I felt a smile come unbidden to my lips. I had taken everything from my ignorant parents. As I gazed down at the signed documents, I looked forward to what the rest of my life would bring.

A few days later, Liam's parents headed to their domain's spaceport, accompanied by some guards. They boarded a specially chartered shuttle, but sat some distance apart. The lavish shuttle would take them into space, where they would board a greater ship that was headed for the Capital Planet in the center of the Empire's vast territory. The capital was far more developed than some count's planet deep in the outskirts.

The two sat without looking at each other; they didn't seem particularly close. While reading an electronic newspaper, Cliff spat, "You got him a *doll?* What kind of mother are you?"

Meanwhile, Darcie drank tea as though she couldn't care less what he had to say. There was no love in their relationship. Their marriage had been one of political convenience.

"That child's nothing more than a product of my genes. How am I supposed to love him with a face like that, and when I didn't even give birth to him myself?"

Liam had been produced artificially using his parents' DNA. To both of them, he was nothing but an heir.

Darcie continued, "Besides, you're one to talk. You think it's okay to just foist everything off onto your five-year-old child?"

"Well, did you want to stay?"

"Are you kidding?" Darcie took another sip of tea, then voiced her many frustrations. "If I hadn't known I'd be able to get out later, I never would have married into this country bumpkin house. We've got no money and nothing but problems. It's just terrible. Of course, I don't feel great about fooling an ignorant child. Giving him that doll was the least I could do, don't you think?"

Cliff smiled. "He'll just be a laughingstock. A noble with a doll at his side? People are going to talk about him behind his back his entire life."

"Whatever, it's got nothing to do with me. I'm done with him now that he's the lord."

Having maid robots—sometimes called dolls—was looked down upon in noble society. It was common for anyone who possessed one to be scorned.

"It'll do him more good than any old servant, though," Darcie said. "It's not like we have any knights or retainers to give him. Plus, if something happens to him, then we'll have to come back, and I do not want that."

"True. Wouldn't want that."

"Is it really okay to just force everything onto a child, though? We're not going to get in trouble for that?" Darcie was more worried about her own future than Liam's.

Cliff grabbed some booze he'd ordered from a crew member and gulped it down. He loosened his collar, clearly feeling relieved to be free of his responsibilities. "Don't worry about it. There's precedent, and I got approval from the Imperial Court. Plenty of people do the same thing, it's fine. Nowadays, nobody cares who's lord, and nobody wants to rule that backwater planet anyway, so who'll complain?"

The Empire had approved of Cliff giving his title and assets to a five-year-old. It was an unusual occurrence, but there was a reason for it.

"The Empire doesn't want anything to do with the boonies either. Long as *somebody's* in charge and doing their duty, they don't care."

The Intergalactic Empire was so vast that it was almost

impossible to govern all of it. It didn't help that the Empire was historically resistant to using artificial intelligence to assist with governance; the use of AI of any type was kept to an absolute minimum. This was because in this world, humanity had nearly been wiped out by the artificial intelligence they'd created. Humanity had once been ruled by AIs, and the people who rose up against them had created the Empire.

Therefore, the nobility didn't approve of things like maid robots, which utilized artificial intelligence. The current trend was that they would be used if needed, but only at a bare minimum.

Darcie looked down at their planet from the shuttle's window—the planet ruled by the House Banfield. It hardly looked like a civilization capable of space travel. The planet's level of development had been forcibly restricted, and the people there lived under a vast amount of debt.

"Liam will probably be furious when he finds out what he's been saddled with."

Cliff was starting to turn a little red from the potent drink. "He'll just push it off onto his own kid and flee to the capital, like me."

A planet no one would be happy ruling over. That was Count Banfield's domain.

◆◇◆

At five years old, I had become a count who ruled over a planet.

"Now that's power. I'm basically a king."

There were many counts in the Empire, so the Banfields were just one of a great number of families of the same rank. But inside my own territory, I was the supreme ruler.

Seated in the chair in my office, which was much too large for my child's body, I received a report from my butler, Brian.

"Your maid robot has arrived, Master Liam."

Brian had served the Banfield family for a long time, and he handled all household matters. He was a slender man approaching old age who maintained his appearance more than adequately for his station. He was the kind of man who would have made me nervous in my past life, but in this one, my authority superseded his, so I spoke down to him even though I was a child.

"Bring her here, then."

"Yes, sir. Come in."

The door to my office opened and the maid robot I had modeled in 3D appeared before me. She strode in gracefully, her posture perfect. I'd been expecting to see a robot that looked just like the image I'd created, but her beauty far exceeded my expectations.

There was nothing unnatural about her movements, nothing about her appearance that screamed "I'm a robot" other than the label on her shoulder that immediately identified her as a maid robot. All of the maid uniform designs featured bare shoulders to make this mark visible. This was necessary as they looked exactly like humans otherwise. She was so well made that I doubted there was any other way than that label to tell she was artificial.

She made her way up to me and performed a gesture that resembled a curtsy, holding up her skirt and bowing. Then she introduced herself in a beautiful voice.

"Pleased to make your acquaintance. I am your Amagi, Master."

I'd been expecting her to sound somewhat unnatural, to have a robotic voice, but she sounded exactly like a human speaking.

I'd named my maid robot "Amagi," which I thought suited her black hair and Japanese looks. Brian hadn't reacted to the name, so it seemed it didn't come across as strange. Apparently, Japanese names weren't completely out of place here, somehow.

"She will take care of you from now on," Brian explained. "However, she'll need to undergo regular maintenance."

"Maintenance?" I glanced at Amagi, who was standing stock-still after finishing her introduction.

"Maintenance is necessary once a week. It should take about two hours," Amagi supplied.

"Huh. I thought she'd run a little longer than that."

Sensing my displeasure, Brian hurriedly told me why maintenance was so important. "The body must be checked every week for irregularities. It gets cleaned as well. If something seriously broke, the manufacturer would have to repair her, so it's important to undergo these checks regularly."

Actually, it was pretty impressive that she could function for a whole week on just two hours of down time.

I turned to Amagi and held my arms out. Sensing my wish, she made her way to me and gently picked up my small body. Her arms around me felt exactly like human arms. I touched her chest, her large breasts far too big to fit into my tiny hands.

"That's ideal softness right there." She had perfect breasts, not too soft and with spring to them.

"Master Liam, you mustn't do such things in front of other people," Brian warned me hesitantly.

Brian had been serving my family for ages, managing the household since my great-grandfather's time. Since the mansion couldn't be maintained without a butler, I couldn't easily fire him, but I was his master. I thought it would be stupid to begin acting like a five-year-old at this point, so I'd decided to abandon all childishness now that I was in charge.

"I'll do exactly as I like. Anyway, what's the status of my domain?"

With a disappointed look on his face, Brian touched the bracelet he wore and holographic images appeared before him, graphs and numbers that represented the state of various parts of my domain. There was a map too, but I didn't know what any of the figures meant.

"I don't get it."

"I don't suppose you would," Brian said, again sounding disappointed.

There was no way I *could* understand it. I mean, in my last life, I had just been a normal salaryman. I had no knowledge of how a territory should be ruled. Plus, this was a society developed enough to have an intergalactic empire. An amateur like me was only going to muck things up with whatever stupid ideas I came up with.

I knew this guy named Arata at my old job who loved isekai stories, but his favorite trope, where the protagonist pulls off hacks with his modern knowledge, wasn't going to come in handy here. Arata was one of those so-called otaku. *I wonder if he's doing well?* He'd taught me a lot, but he quit the company before I was forced to leave, so I remembered him fondly as one of the people who hadn't disparaged me. *I should have talked to him more.*

This is a problem, though... I have no idea what to do. That could very well mean I'm unable to do anything. Nothing good, and nothing bad either, putting my "evil lord" aspirations on hold.

While I was pondering this in Amagi's arms and fondling her breasts, she spoke up, "Master, I am equipped with functions to assist in governance. Would you care for my assistance?"

"Really? I have no clue what to do. Can you even help me at this stage?"

"Of course," replied Amagi. "I would recommend utilizing an education capsule. In the meantime, I will manage your domain in your stead. You may think of it as an emergency tactic."

Brian's face paled. It seemed he didn't agree with the suggestion. "You mustn't! The Empire will not accept management by an AI. They are only permitted to provide support!"

Amagi replied coolly, "The Empire has no such law. Utilizing artificial intelligence as little as possible is simply preferred. As Master does not possess the knowledge for governance, I have merely suggested the most efficient option. However, I will only do as Master commands."

Both Amagi and Brian looked to me. Have her rule while I studied in an education capsule, eh?

Education capsules were incredibly convenient devices. Once you were submerged in the liquid inside them, they would install knowledge directly into your brain. They would also strengthen the body. In one such capsule, the equivalent of elementary and junior high education could be accomplished in half a year. It was a miraculous invention that compressed nine years of learning into six months. The only drawback was that even if the capsule drilled knowledge into you and enhanced your physical strength, these attributes wouldn't stick if you ceased to use them after you came out. It was like how you could carry around a dictionary, but if you didn't use it, it was meaningless.

You needed to undergo some physical therapy after you left the capsule as well. Since you came out of it physically different than when you went in, if you didn't train to acclimate yourself to your new body, it could be dangerous just living life as normal. Also, you were basically sleeping the whole time you were in the capsule; you couldn't do anything else. Still, it was endlessly more efficient than regular studying.

I can't do anything now, when I don't know what any of these numbers and graphs mean. If that's the case...then there's really only one choice to be made.

"Brian, ready the capsule. Amagi, I put you in charge of my territory while I'm in there."

"Master Liam! You can't!" Brian shouted.

Amagi simply said, "As you command."

It seems she won't listen to orders from anyone but me. That's wonderful. A far cry from a flesh-and-blood woman. However, I will try to persuade Brian, even if it is annoying.

"Listen, Brian. You don't want me making decisions about things when I don't know what I'm doing, right? This is necessary."

"P-perhaps, but think of the scandal..."

"It's just for a little while. If you understand me, then get it ready."

Plus, if I can leave these matters to someone else, that's fine with me. I don't care about their hang-ups about artificial intelligence.

Damn, though... I didn't think I'd have to study just to exploit my subjects. Oh well, I'll play nice for a while. I am still a child in body, after all. Even if one day I'll torment my subjects and extort taxes from them, I wouldn't want to do it as a kid.

I thought such things as I fondled Amagi's breasts.

The domain of Count Banfield was in fact significantly *less* culturally advanced than Liam's previous world. For one thing, there was no reason for its ruler to ensure its people lived comfortable lives.

Since they had education capsules at their disposal, if the lord had wanted highly knowledgeable personnel, he could have simply recruited anyone and given them the education they would need. From its ruler's perspective, all the planet required was a sufficient population to work without complaint and pay their taxes. And House Banfield wasn't the only one. There were some lords in the Empire who forced their people to live at medieval levels of civilization. To the citizens of their territories, the nobility had absolute authority.

The people who had long been ruled by the Banfields had just learned they had a new ruler, and they were rather anxious at this news. In one particular town, the mood was dark and uneasy. Inside a seedy old bar, a weary-looking bartender conversed with another man who had stopped in on his way home from work. The topic of conversation? Liam, of course.

"D'you hear? The new lord's a tender five years of age. There's being too young and then there's *that*, am I right?"

Glancing down at the glass he was drying, the bartender replied, "They might increase taxes 'cause of these changes too."

It had been bad when Cliff had taken over. That had been *hundreds* of years ago at this point, but since it wasn't unusual for people to live several centuries in this world, the bartender still remembered.

"The last guy used his taking the reins as an excuse to collect some pretty ridiculous taxes."

The last two Count Banfields had both been terrible lords. Liam's great-grandfather had actually been a good ruler, but there were no traces left of his legacy now. The two lords who had followed him had squandered all the riches he'd amassed. Now only the elderly told stories of how people in the past had lived blessed lives. The newer generations knew only hardship.

Gulping down the cheap booze that would quickly get him drunk, the patron also voiced his frustrations. "Are we just livestock for those nobles?"

"You shouldn't speak so loudly. Let's just hope this new lord's a good one."

"Do you really think that?"

"Hey, it's not impossible. Though it's probably pretty close."

"How am I supposed to hope...?" the customer muttered, laying his head down on the bar.

None of Liam's subjects had any hope for him.

I'M THE **EVIL LORD** OF AN
THE
INTERGALACTIC
EMPIRE

2 Sword Master

TWO YEARS HAD PASSED since Liam had taken over his domain.

Brian, House Banfield's butler, privately lamented again today as he walked through the mansion. The house, which had been rebuilt two generations prior by Count Banfield—Liam's grandfather—was eccentric, to put it mildly. To be honest, it was in poor taste. When visitors arrived, they would grimace and endeavor not to bring up the house in conversation. Many of them would wear strained smiles on their faces. The halls twisted and turned in an almost labyrinthine fashion. It was common for newly hired servants to get lost in them.

As Brian turned a corner, he found some servants chatting in an inconspicuous spot. It was a young man and woman. The man was a gardener, but he'd left the yard in the hands of a machine and was slacking off, hitting on one of the maids in her short-skirted uniform.

"Come on, it's fine, isn't it?"

"We'll get in trouble if they find us."

"They won't. There are plenty of unused rooms."

"Yeah, true... Just keep it a secret, okay?"

The man put his arm around the maid's shoulder and the two of them left, blowing off their work. They didn't change their behavior when they saw Brian, nor did they greet him. The previous count, Cliff, had prioritized appearances when hiring servants, ignoring capability and personality. For that reason, the mansion was filled with workers of low character, leaving Brian frustrated.

"What would Master Alistair say if he saw this?"

Things had once been different. When Brian had first started with the Banfields, they'd had a proper mansion and servants who took their job seriously. Liam's great-grandfather, Alistair Sera Banfield, had been a wise ruler, and Brian had been proud to serve him. Things had started to get rough when Liam's grandfather took over. From then on, the situation had deteriorated quickly. House Banfield's debts rose as quickly as its reputation fell, plunging the family into a dark age.

The count had lived a life of utmost luxury, burning through the family's assets while levying harsh taxes on the people to squeeze as much as he could from them. He was unable to give up the life he was accustomed to, and even he went into debt. Then, when his debts became too much to handle, he forced everything onto the next Count Banfield, Cliff, and fled to the Capital Planet like a fool. Having been raised by such a father, Cliff turned out no better.

As he lamented the state of House Banfield, which no longer resembled the family he'd originally served, Brian arrived at the count's office and adjusted his uniform, straightening his back.

The device next to the door lit up and transmitted his voice into the room. "Master Liam, it's Brian."

Liam's voice came from the device. "Come in."

The steady voice, which didn't seem like it had come from a young boy, made the butler a little nervous. Brian opened the door and entered the room to find Liam sitting at his desk assessing the state of his domain, Amagi at his side. Amagi supported Liam in a secretary-like role. Liam was upset, irritation plain on his face. It was an expression Brian could hardly believe a child's face capable of.

"What can I do for you, Master Liam?"

The office's desk had been made for an adult, but a child's chair had been provided for Liam. Climbing down from that chair, Liam joined his hands behind his back and paced about the room, looking like a child playing at being important. In actuality, Liam *was* quite important. Though a child, he was a count and lord of a domain, and no one on this planet could speak out against him.

"Brian, I've never been outside the mansion before."

"Indeed. The mansion is equipped with all facilities for the education and physical therapy you receive, after all."

Up until recently, Liam had been sleeping inside the education capsule. Instead of the usual six months, he'd spent a full year inside, acquiring a thorough education and physical enhancement. Then, when he'd left the capsule, there had been physical rehabilitation and a review of the knowledge he'd gained waiting for him.

If he wanted to go outside, there were inner courtyards for him to use, so there had never been a need for him to actually leave the mansion. He still didn't need to, which was why Liam hadn't previously noticed how bad the house he lived in looked.

"I was curious, so I finally went outside. This mansion... It looks awful, doesn't it?"

Brian agreed, but as his butler, he couldn't speak ill of his earlier master's taste. "I would say it has a creative design."

"Spare me your flattery!" Liam shouted, stamping his little feet. He shot a look at Amagi and a projection of the mansion his grandfather and father had built appeared before them. The main house, a vacation home, and various other buildings hovered in holographic form around Liam. They were all terribly shaped, each building completely lacking in design sense, even seeming to give off some sort of ill will.

"Are you stupid? You've gotta be stupid, right? Why the obsession with strange shapes? It's humiliating to live in this thing! Aren't you embarrassed? *I'm* embarrassed!"

I'm relieved that Master Liam has normal tastes. Brian felt a twinge of happiness at that.

It didn't change the fact that their estate was full of terribly shaped buildings. Some of these buildings had been set aside for relatives of the Banfields, but knowing of the family's current financial situation, the relatives in question had all fled for the Capital Planet already. No one lived in them.

Another of the reasons Liam had so easily taken over the family was that none of these relatives had been around to object to it. Then again, no one wanted a territory like this. The family hadn't had vassals or knights for generations.

Knights were much more powerful warriors than ordinary rank-and-file soldiers, forged through training to have practically inhuman strength. The majority of these individuals served nations or lords within the Empire. Possessed of many talents, these mighty warriors were not just skilled fighters, but served as commanders as well. However, not a single one of them served House Banfield. As for the reason why, they'd either learned of the family's financial troubles and gone off to serve other lords, or they'd obeyed Liam's grandfather's orders and followed him to the Capital Planet. As such, Liam had no knights in his employ.

When it came to government officials, general military personnel, and servants... There wasn't an abundance, but Liam had enough. It was just these exemplary individuals whom he lacked.

It breaks my heart, thought Brian. *Leaving everything to such a young child and fleeing to the capital would have been unthinkable in Master Alistair's time.*

"We'll demolish the whole estate," Liam declared. "I don't want this mansion. I'll build a new one that suits me better."

"Wh-what about those employed to maintain the other mansions and villas?" Brian responded, somewhat flustered.

Liam's irritated response was: "I don't care. Fire them."

Just fire them outright? Brian thought, but Amagi offered a comforting suggestion.

"Master, we should provide new employment for the servants. Also, I suggest waiting a little before constructing a new mansion."

"Why's that?"

"I agree with demolishing the estate, to reduce the cost of maintaining it. However, building a mansion that suits you will take time. Therefore, I suggest first building a residence that functions at the most basic level while your proper mansion is being readied."

Brian was relieved to hear the suggestion.

I guess it's better than accruing more debts. But won't it cost a lot to demolish everything? Still, in the long run, that's better than paying to maintain these ridiculously huge buildings.

Liam pondered for a short time, then agreed with Amagi's proposal with a nod.

"You're right. We should take our time building the perfect mansion. Where will we get the money, though?"

Amagi was quick to provide another suggestion. "I believe restructuring the army would suffice."

"The army?"

The Empire allowed the lords personal armies for the

defense of their domains. Liam had only just begun to get a sense of the state of his territory, so he didn't know much about his army yet. Amagi showed him some data, and he reacted with fascination.

"We've got thirty thousand battleships? That's a lot!"

Amagi nodded. "Yes. However, less than 20 percent of these ships are operational."

They had thirty thousand ships but couldn't even use six thousand of them. They were all fairly old models too, so their army was actually a lot more bark than bite.

"The current number of ships is unnecessary, so we should cut them down to a number we can realistically maintain. I suggest a minimum of three thousand ships, which would drastically reduce the cost of maintaining the army."

Brian was shocked at Amagi's suggestion. "A-a mere three thousand?"

Liam was having a hard time wrapping his head around these numbers. "Is that a lot, or no? I'm not sure how to decide."

"Please wait!" Brian cut in, reluctant to see Amagi's suggestion approved. "A count is generally expected to maintain an army of ten thousand ships. I advise against reducing our forces to a mere 10 percent!"

Liam cocked his head. "But only 20 percent of them are even operational."

It was true that their fleet's current operability was too low, but visibly reducing the size of the army had its own problems. Brian said, "The operability is not the only issue. If we reduce the size of our army, those around us will take us that much less seriously as a result, and it won't just be the nobility. Pirates will come running!"

Reducing the army to a tenth of its size would give other nobles more cause to look down on the family for its financial situation. It wasn't unheard of for neighboring lords to go to war even within the Empire. Being held in low estimation would make House Banfield vulnerable.

There was another troublesome group in this world: pirates. Space pirates, to be more specific. They were so troublesome, in fact, that some large pirate armadas were more than a match for ruling lords. A large army was a good deterrent for such foes. No pirate would bother attacking a territory protected by thirty thousand ships.

However, Amagi had a counterargument ready. "Currently, we would need a thousand of our ships to go up against a fleet of a hundred pirate ships, due to the age of our equipment and the skill of our soldiers. Rather than continue with such an inefficient army, I believe we should reduce the scale of our forces while increasing the utility of our personnel."

Liam made his decision quickly. "We'll reduce our army, then." He accepted Amagi's proposal despite Brian's stark opposition.

"Master Liaaam!" Tears welled up in Brian's eyes, but Liam wouldn't hear his objections.

"I don't need people I can't use."

Amagi swiftly drew up the plans to reduce the size of the army. "We will begin the reorganization immediately. This should provide us with a fairly robust budget."

"What a pointless display. Twenty-four thousand ships we can't even use except as decorations."

Brian was starting to get anxious. Liam accepted suggestions from AI all too easily. "Master Liam, you're relying on artificial intelligence too much! You must use this machine, not be used by them! Other noble houses will believe House Banfield is in decline."

Liam snorted. "You talk like the family *isn't* in decline. If you don't have a better suggestion, then keep quiet."

Brian's shoulders slumped. Of course he didn't have any suggestions. He was only a butler, after all. He had no place in discussions of political or military affairs.

Looking at Amagi, Liam said, "Having too few forces won't be good, though. I can't make light of our military situation. Will we be able to bring our numbers back up eventually?"

This caused Brian to revise his opinion of Liam once more. *What? He's giving it more thought than I imagined.*

Amagi nodded. It seemed reducing the size of the military wasn't her entire plan. "Eventually, we will amass a force befitting a count's army. We will begin with reeducation and retraining to create an elite force, then increase the number of our troops as the financial situation of the territory improves."

She suggested removing excess personnel from the military and putting them in civilian jobs to stimulate the planet's economy.

Liam agreed with her reasoning. "I don't need an army that's just for display. What I do need is an army that can fight. Go ahead with the reorganization, Amagi. One day, we'll turn it into an armada befitting a count—no, befitting *me*."

He asked Brian, "Any complaints? We'll have thirty thousand ships again eventually, but we'll make do with three thousand for now."

Brian wiped the sweat from his brow with a handkerchief. "N-no complaints, Master Liam."

Satisfied with Brian's response, Liam turned back to Amagi. "Carry it out at once, Amagi."

"Yes, Master."

This decisiveness even as a child... He almost reminds me of Master Alistair, Brian thought. He was starting to see some similarities between Liam and the brilliant lord he'd once served. However...

"Well, that's one problem solved. Amagi, up."

"Yes, Master."

His tendency to enjoy being held in the arms of his doll, Amagi, even in front of others, was not something Brian could commend. In his mind, he complained, *Master Liam, please do not sit in Amagi's arms and fondle her breasts in my presence. I have no clue what sort of expression to make!*

Things were more dire than I had expected. When I got out of the education capsule, finished my rehabilitation, and got a look at the state of my domain, I was rendered speechless. Thanks to the knowledge installed in my brain, when I saw the data, I was able to comprehend what it all meant, whether I wanted to or not. And because I understood, that made it all the worse.

"Exploit my subjects... These people don't even have anything for me to exploit!"

The world I had reincarnated into was one with a highly advanced scientific and magical civilization—or at least, it was supposed to be. In truth, the people on this planet had a less-developed civilization than Japan, where I'd lived my previous life. At worst, they were about at the level of pre-war Japan.

This was an intergalactic civilization, a world where space battleships shot beams at one another in war, yet it seemed like my territory alone had been completely left behind by the times. There was no energy to the people living here either. They just barely managed to pay their taxes. Even if I wanted to oppress them, they couldn't be any more oppressed than they already were. It was like a land that had already been bled dry by an evil lord, and I hadn't even done anything yet.

"Why is the civilization here so far behind?" I griped.

Amagi explained the reason matter-of-factly. "Cultural development occurs with no effort. It would be easy for the nobility to leave the people to their own devices. However, if civilization develops too much, it becomes more difficult to manage."

Is that why? "Then manage with artificial intelligence!"

"We do, and it does as much as it can under the prescribed 'minimum use' rules."

The nobles in this world bled taxes from their

citizens and allowed them to achieve as little cultural development as possible. If they left their people alone, the population increased, and if they needed workers with intelligence from that pool, they could simply toss them into a capsule for education. They kept the people just oppressed enough that they didn't acquire too much knowledge. There was no room for me to do anything. My time as an evil lord was over before it had even begun!

"Did my parents just force a completely worthless domain on me?"

Could the Guide have tricked me? The thought went through my head, but Amagi was there to set me straight.

"Master, it is true that House Banfield's domain is in a rather sorry state, but I believe things can only get better from here. If you make good use of the taxes, you will see results in another ten or twenty years."

People lived long lives in this world. They didn't reach adulthood until fifty, and at fifty, they looked like someone around thirteen in my old world. There was still war, which affected the average life expectancy to some degree, but I had learned it was still around three hundred to four hundred years. Plenty of people lived to be six hundred. From that standpoint, twenty years seemed rather brief.

"Twenty years, huh?"

"Yes. In twenty years, you can advance civilization in your territory."

If Amagi says so, then I suppose that's that. I'll see how things go, then...for twenty years. It won't be any fun exploiting my people as they are now. My body is still young. I've got plenty of time, so I'll just invest in my domain for now and reap the rewards later.

"Put everything but the bare minimum funds into maintaining the planet. I'll take it back later. And Amagi—I want power."

While I was biding my time, there were all sorts of things I wanted to obtain.

"Power? The military—"

"No. Personal power. My own power."

"Your own? You wish to train your body?"

"That's right. I want to become strong, through martial arts or something like that."

Violence had frightened me in my past life. I was afraid of the burly men who came to collect on my debts. Before that, I'd always thought violence was meaningless, but after landing in that situation, I began to feel you really did need physical power.

In order to rule with an iron fist, I wanted power, enough that I wouldn't have to fear anyone. The power to enact violence on whomever I wished, hence my desire for a strong body.

"I do not believe such a thing is necessary for you, Master. The bare minimum training would suffice, in my opinion."

"No. Find me a top-class instructor, and don't skimp on the budget. This is a necessary expense."

In order for me to hold on to what was mine...

In order for me to be the victimizer instead of the victim... I needed *power*.

In what could be called the threshold between worlds...

Everything was dark, nothing visible nearby. The only thing in this space was the grinning Guide. He sat on his travel bag as if it were placed on solid ground and happily watched an image hovering before him. In the image was the haggard figure of Liam's ex-wife, several years later—his ex-wife in his previous life, that is. She was walking down the street, exhaustion written on her face.

"Looking very worn-out, there. Your hair's a mess, and your clothes look cheap and shabby."

She was working through her savings, barely managing to support herself and her daughter. The Guide was satisfied at how much the woman had changed. All around him were similar images of other people in distress, people he'd personally brought misfortune. The negative emotions of those people filled him up. He felt power welling within him.

"Oops, can't be getting all my kicks from a bonus like you. I should check in on Liam. Oh, I'm so busy."

Busy as he claimed to be, he was enjoying himself to his heart's content. He reached out his hand and a new image appeared. It revealed a seven-year-old Liam conversing with his doll.

The Guide chuckled. "Unable to trust in flesh-and-blood women, he's put an elaborately made doll at his side. It's hilarious. Plus, he doesn't seem to have realized this is putting his status as a noble at risk. What an amusing situation." Best of all was that Liam didn't seem to realize the misery of his situation.

"I might as well take my time savoring—oh?"

In the projected image, Liam was saying that he wanted power. A person who'd been afraid of violence in their past life wanting power in their new one—the Guide couldn't get enough.

"He wants power to hold on to what's his, eh? Typical! But that's what's so good about it!"

The Guide touched the projection with his hand. Black smoke wafted from his body and seeped into the image.

"I know the perfect person for your needs. Don't worry, I'll keep watching over you. This is an ongoing service, after all."

The Guide pulled some strings of fate—tugged them, really—to find the man who would instruct Liam. Once he'd done this, the man was guaranteed to fill the position. Liam had requested a skilled teacher, yet this man was anything but.

"Enjoy, Liam. When you meet your doom, I'll be sure to come and collect you."

The Guide wore his crescent-moon smile, only his mouth visible in his face.

A solo traveler arrived at House Banfield's spaceport. He was an aged man in a kimono and purple hakama, with messy hair and a scruffy face. A katana rested at his hip.

"Out in the middle of nowhere, this place."

The man's name was Yasushi, and despite his sloppy appearance, he had come to teach Liam martial arts. However, it wasn't truly Yasushi who was supposed to be there. They had requested a real martial arts master, but the man in question had "coincidentally" learned of House Banfield's misdeeds and thus hadn't wanted to accept the request. For that matter, he didn't even know if House Banfield could pay the fee they were offering. Therefore, the original master had volunteered Yasushi for the job instead.

"Dammit... If only I hadn't borrowed money from that guuuuy!"

The sight of Yasushi lamenting with slumped shoulders was rather pathetic. He didn't appear in the slightest like a man in possession of martial prowess. Yasushi had accepted the job on the condition that his debts would be canceled, but when he saw the deserted, run-down spaceport, he started to regret the decision.

"I wouldn't want to come here even for my real job."

Frankly speaking, this man was not strong. He'd studied all sorts of martial arts but hadn't managed to stick with any one of them for very long. Instead, he merely boasted of having mastered the martial arts and made his living by showing off techniques that boiled down to magic tricks.

"Well, the client's a kid, so it should be easy enough to fool him, but I almost feel bad that he has to learn how to fight from me."

Yasushi *had* learned the basics, so he'd be capable of teaching the boy, but the basics were all he could teach him. He wouldn't be able to impart any advanced techniques or killer moves, as he didn't know any. In all honesty, even his grasp on the basics was starting to slip at this point. The only reason he'd accepted the job in spite of all this was because he needed the money.

"Well, it'll work out."

A bratty kid would get tired of it quickly, he figured. If he praised the kid enough and kept him in a good mood, that would probably satisfy him.

"The katana, though... I tried dressing to look the part, but what a strange kid to make these requests."

Katanas existed in this world, but they were not what one would consider mainstream. They would never fall out of popularity within a certain niche, but the vast majority of swordsmen preferred Western blades. It had been a long time since Yasushi had held one.

"Welp, time to trick a kid out of his money."

This man's true profession was the performing arts. He'd only been chosen as Liam's instructor through the Guide's machinations.

3 The Way of the Flash

AN OLD MAN with an odd vibe about him had shown up.

The man—Master Yasushi—sat across from me in the mansion courtyard, his legs folded under him. He looked serene, seated there on the grass. His unshaven face and shabby kimono made him seem like a masterless samurai or something, but the air he gave off was slightly different. In any case, I supposed this was what a true master of martial arts looked like.

"Lord Liam." Master said my name, slowly and quietly.

"Y-yes!" I shrank back a little, but he gave me a smile.

"There is no need to be nervous. First, let me explain to you the school of swordsmanship to which I belong."

Master showed me his sword. I knew that katanas existed in this world, so I figured if I was going to learn something, it might as well be that. No deep thought had gone into the decision, but it was looking like I'd chosen well. *If I can learn from someone like this, I was right to pick the katana.*

"The school of swordsmanship I use has a secret technique, Lord Liam. It is not something I can show just anyone, but I'm sure you wish to see my true ability. In which case, I will reveal this technique, just once. However, no one outside our school may see it. Only you, Lord Liam."

I hadn't expected him to start with a secret technique. I figured that was something he'd be more protective of, but he had a kindness to him, and he seemed very serious about teaching me. *Master must be quite an upstanding person.*

However, standing behind me, Amagi was giving Master a rather distrustful look. "For Liam's safety, I cannot allow that."

"You're being rude, Amagi." I scolded her, but Amagi wouldn't budge.

"Your safety is my first priority."

Master didn't seem at all perturbed. He merely stated, quietly but firmly, "Then I will not be able to accept this job."

He was so calm, even in front of a count! This guy was the real deal, practically oozing confidence in his own strength. *I want to learn from him!*

"Amagi, I will allow it!"

Unable to oppose my fierce determination, Amagi reluctantly acquiesced. "If anything should happen, please call for help immediately. Take this as well."

"What is it?" She'd handed me a device.

"There are many swordsmen who are swindlers. Please use this to investigate him."

"Investigate?"

"Yes. It detects devices used in fraud. I trust you do not mind?" Amagi directed her gaze at Master, but he just sat there smiling.

"I don't mind."

"I will watch from a distance, then. Master, please be careful."

Amagi went off, leaving me alone with my master, who stood and handed me one of a number of logs he'd prepared earlier.

"You're going to cut this?" It was just a regular old log. The fraud detector didn't show any reaction to it.

"Yes, that's right. We'll start by placing these in areas my sword can't reach. I'll leave their placement to you, Lord Liam."

I designated locations for these logs, and Master stood them up on the ground accordingly, until they were all around him in different spots. They were far enough away that he couldn't reach them even if he drew his katana, one being over five meters away from him.

Master began to explain his method, his sword still in its scabbard. "Lord Liam, the secret technique of the Way of the Flash is the height of martial prowess, and it utilizes magic as well. This is the only technique you will need. As for the rest, you need only focus on the basics."

I gulped, awed by my master's presence. The swordsmanship of this world was *fantasy* swordsmanship. In a world where people could slash their swords while ignoring the laws of physics, to only have one particular technique was a rather extreme style. The Way of the Flash, huh? It must have been an incredible art.

"You must not reveal this technique to just anyone. However, if you master it, it will not matter if someone witnesses it. This is the secret technique—the Flash."

Master took his left thumb and pushed up the guard of his sword, then let it fall back with a satisfying *clink*. That was the only motion I saw as he stood there, posture relaxed.

"What's wrong, Master?" I asked, thinking his silence odd, but then I heard a log falling behind me and turned toward it.

"No way..." All the logs had been cut and were lying in segments on the ground. The cuts were clean, all the logs having been sliced in different places.

They weren't close enough for his sword to reach, so is it something swift and fluid like iaido? But when did he draw his sword? I didn't see it. While I was puzzling over everything, Master took a deep breath.

"This is the signature technique of the Way of the Flash."

I quickly looked down at the device, but nothing happened. "When did you cut them?"

In response to my surprised question, Master snapped his sword for me once more. Another log was sliced, the one standing right behind him. The device didn't react at all, not detecting any signs of fraud, and I stared up at him in awe.

"You'll understand as you learn the Way of the Flash. Finding the answer yourself is part of the training. Let me ask, then: do you wish to learn the Way of the Flash?"

Of course I do! I gave him a big nod. "Yes!"

This fantasy world's amazing! I didn't expect there to be such an amazing move! If I can master this, I'll grow stronger for sure!

This kid's easy to fool, Yasushi thought as he looked down at Liam, who stood before him with eyes aglitter.

He felt a little guilty tricking such a young child, but he had to make a living somehow. *Pretty unfortunate for him that he has to learn from an amateur.*

He was putting on an air of importance for Liam, but the man was by no means a master of the blade. All air and no substance...that was Yasushi.

Well, nobles are all rotten anyway. I'll make as much money off this kid as I can.

He eyed the logs he'd "cut." The technique he'd used to make himself look masterful was simple sleight of hand. All the logs had already been cut, save for the one he'd given to Liam, which he'd then switched for another.

Don't judge me later, kid. It's your fault for not picking up on such a simple trick. Yasushi glanced at the device in Liam's hand and gave a quick sigh of relief. *Phew, I was a little nervous there. I'm glad that didn't go off. If it had, I would've said it was just 'cause I used magic, but... Is it broken or something? Oh, whatever.*

In fact, the fraud detector Liam was using had one flaw: it would react to signs of sophisticated deception, but not primitive sleight of hand. In other words, the device hadn't picked up on Yasushi's trick because it was too simple.

"Let's get started on the basics, then," Yasushi told Liam.

"Yes, Master!"

As he looked down at this child, who didn't doubt him for a minute, Yasushi chuckled to himself.

It had been three years since Yasushi had begun teaching Liam swordplay. Liam practiced the basics almost every day, and Yasushi watched him from afar.

"Kids sure learn quick. I'm jealous. What should I teach him next?"

Yasushi had taught Liam the basics of not only the katana, but short swords, spears, and a number of other weapons, plus unarmed fighting. He'd sold it to Liam as "learning the characteristics of other weapons." There was only so much Yasushi could teach him, however. Mostly, he found free videos of entry-level martial arts knowhow and passed those on to Liam. He parroted impressive-sounding quotes from famous people, and the kid found his own meaning in them. All in all, he was having a pretty easy time of it.

Resting in the shade of a tree, Yasushi looked over at the new "mansion." The unique building that had stood there previously had been demolished, and a very simple house had been built in its place. It was such a modest structure that you never would've guessed it was the dwelling of a count.

"There're lots of nasty rumors about House Banfield, but he does seem to be living pretty frugally." Liam's treatment of Yasushi was by no means bad either. In fact, the count seemed to value the man so much that it was almost a letdown.

"I thought nobles were supposed to be slothful and domineering, but that kid's pretty serious." Liam was different from what Yasushi had expected. Today, he was once again practicing diligently.

"I don't see the point in a noble training like this. Won't his subordinates protect him anyway?" Yasushi yawned. But there was no problem with it. Well, there was one problem.

In a mere three years, Yasushi was already running out of things to teach Liam. The boy practiced the basics earnestly and learned quickly. To be honest, he was now stronger than Yasushi. Now if Yasushi were to execute an unskilled move or make a badly thought-out comment, he was worried the boy would be able to see through him. This was why he presently just watched over Liam.

"This isn't hard, but that doll observes us every so often. Why the heck does he have one of those things, anyway?" Nobles typically wanted nothing to do with dolls. Even if they happened to own one, they only did so in secret. That was another reason Yasushi found Liam so odd, though he had a rough guess as to the kid's reasons.

"Giving peerage and territory to a kid who doesn't know anything... Nobles sure do some awful shit." Yasushi just assumed that, having been raised in an insulated environment, Liam wasn't wise to the ways of this world. "But his domain's developing because of it. How ironic."

Over the past couple of years, Liam's lifeless planet had started to get a little of its energy back. Former soldiers and other people of his domain who'd undergone job training were now working to improve the planet's infrastructure. Dormant facilities had been revitalized, and more tax money than ever was going back into the territory. Despite this, the family's debts were as massive as ever, and they were still short on funds.

"Poor kid. He's working so hard without knowing a thing. Almost brings a tear to my eye." Yasushi felt a touch of sympathy for the boy—but that was it, really. He didn't intend to tell him he was being swindled, not when there was still money to be made. There was one thing that was bothering Yasushi, though.

"I bet that kid hates corruption. He might erase me if he finds out the truth."

Liam was a rather serious type among nobles. If he uncovered corruption, what would he do? This was Yasushi's sole concern at the moment.

Shortly after I started learning martial arts, my new mansion was completed. I was expecting something a lot simpler, but from my point of view, it was still fairly impressive.

"Maybe this will be good enough?" It had been meant as a temporary mansion, but I ended up satisfied with it. It was plenty big, with tall ceilings. It wasn't unique or eccentric, just a normal mansion that would cause me no inconvenience to live in.

I was signing documents in my new office when Amagi asked me about my future plans.

"Master, when would you next like to enter the capsule?"

"Is it that time already?" A person had to use the education capsules in stages. You couldn't just go into one for decades and complete your whole education; you had to make use of them in a number of sessions before reaching adulthood. "When should I?"

"Whenever you'd like. Your next session should take six months."

"I'll go in soon, then. While I'm inside, I'll leave ruling to you."

We continued working quietly until Amagi came upon one document in particular. Studying the electronic record floating in the air, she suddenly started checking several others as well.

"What is it?"

"Please look at this document."

It had been cleverly concealed, but there were clear signs that the figures in one official's report had been doctored. Embezzlement.

"Summon whoever submitted this." My voice was lower than usual.

Amagi bowed. "Very well."

A few hours after Amagi contacted him, one of the higher-ranking officials of my domain reported to my mansion.

The man wore an expensive-looking suit over his protruding stomach. He wore rings adorned with gems on every one of his fingers. This man projected an image of wealth, broadcasting it so loudly as to be obnoxious and completely tasteless. Not even I could have worn something like that.

He stood before me with a grin on his face that irritated me to no end. "My lord, I'm sure you cannot yet understand this, but these are simply the necessary expenses of my work. The numbers on the documents are not everything."

This went on for some time as he rattled off countless excuses for the discrepancies in the document. Since I didn't know how valid any of his claims were, I sought Amagi's opinion. Artificial intelligence was handy at times like this. Without petty emotions, AIs prioritized simple efficiency.

"There is clear evidence of embezzlement, not to mention other crimes. The embezzlement alone is nothing but a hindrance to upkeep of the domain's facilities, of course, but there are also many expenditures which cannot possibly be called necessary."

I took the electronic document Amagi had prepared for me and looked it over. It had much to say about the official standing before me. I was almost impressed that he was able to stand in front of me and smile. In addition to embezzlement, he'd manipulated human resources, paid bribes...everything you'd expect from your typical corrupt official. Hell, I had a lot to learn from this guy, aside from his fashion choices.

One of the items on the list caught my eye. It said he'd erased one of his subordinates. He'd pinned his embezzlement on this man and executed him and his entire family. When I saw that, I decided what to do with this official.

The sight of him standing there, scarlet-faced, as he attempted to lecture me was almost comical. "You mustn't trust what dolls say, my lord. They're the ones who almost destroyed human civilization. They're humanity's enemy! You're being deceived, my lord. True, I may have bent the rules here and there, but everyone does it. It's necessary to grease the wheels of a job like this, and dolls can't understand that!"

I ignored the official's lecture. I couldn't care less what he had to say. He'd reawakened memories that were practically boiling me from the inside. These memories alone were enough to piss me off.

"Did you enjoy killing your subordinate? What did it feel like, pinning your crimes on him?"

"H-huh?"

"I'm asking, do you enjoy living your life after blaming your crimes on an innocent man?"

"I-I don't know what you're talking about."

When I saw the sweat breaking out on the official's face, I recalled my former boss, the one who'd pinned his embezzlement on me. I saw his face superimposed on the official in front of me. It irritated me to no end.

The man's eyes darted about as I glared silently at him. "I-I suppose something like that may have happened..."

I placed my hand on the handle of the sword I'd taken to carrying around with me. Seeing that, Amagi stepped forward to stop me.

"You mustn't, Master!"

I drew my sword, and the official dropped all pretenses, finally telling me how he really felt.

"Wh-who do you think keeps you alive, boy? You only live like this because we support—"

He was still yelling when I leapt at him and brought my sword down, cutting him in half. It only took a moment. After I'd bisected him, the official still wore a look of bewilderment, as if he couldn't understand what had happened.

I was young, but I'd undergone physical strengthening and trained for three years. Killing a person was a simple task for me. The fruits of my efforts were clearly apparent. Blood sprayed from the halved official, dirtying my reception room, which just agitated me further. I felt that I shouldn't have called him here.

"Shut your disgusting mouth."

Amagi approached me and sprayed me with a cleansing foam. The foam quickly dissipated, taking the blood on my clothes and skin along with it.

"Master, he is already dead," she pointed out.

Hearing that, I regained a little of my cool. My emotions had gone a bit off the rails there. Even so, as I continued to stare down at the official's corpse, I felt the anger bubbling up inside me once more. I'd cut him down because of his striking similarity to my boss in my previous life.

"The only one allowed to use *my* authority is *me*! Garbage like this can die! Amagi, I want a thorough investigation. I'm executing every single one of these corrupt officials!"

I don't mind valuing the people who serve me well, but I won't allow anyone to make me their puppet. I'm the only one allowed to oppress my people!

"Master, please let go." Amagi gently wrapped her hands around mine as they gripped my sword. I tried to release it, but my fingers wouldn't budge.

"H-huh?"

"Allow me to help."

She pulled each one of my fingers away from the handle of my sword. When I finally let go of it, I realized I was sweating profusely. *Am I feeling guilt over killing a person for the first time?* If that was true, it was awfully pathetic for someone who aimed to become an evil lord.

Amagi took my sword from me, cleaned off the blood, and returned it to its scabbard.

"Regarding your earlier directive: if every corrupt official is disposed of, the chain of command will collapse."

"Are there that many of them?"

"Yes. Corruption has been rampant for quite some time now. I can act as a substitute, but I do not think that will be enough for normal functions to continue."

I don't want Amagi to have to shoulder all that herself either. "So what's the solution?"

"I would suggest employing several dolls suitable for their tasks, though they do not have to be as sophisticated as me. That, or utilizing an artificial intelligence specialized in management."

Artificial intelligence would be way more useful than these guys, I thought as I looked down at the official again and listened to Amagi's proposal. The problem was what society would think of it. *It's like Brian told me— extensive use of artificial intelligence is frowned upon in the Empire. But that's got nothing to do with me, so why should I worry? After all, I'm going to be an evil lord.* I didn't care what society thought, but I could at least keep up appearances. I'd just have to use artificial intelligence alongside humans.

"How many do we need?"

Amagi was quick to answer. "Thirty mass-produced units at minimum. The mansion still needs to be managed, after all. An additional unit specialized in governing as well as its auxiliary units should suffice."

Most people in this world think artificial intelligence will betray you, so it can't be trusted. To that I say, "So what?" Humans will betray you too. No, humans are less trustworthy. I'll go with Amagi's proposal.

"Handle it."

"Are you sure, Master? It will affect your standing."

"I don't care. I trust you more than *these* guys." I gestured at the now-silent official.

"I will make the arrangements."

I narrowed my eyes and said, in a voice so low it surprised even me, "I don't need anyone who defies me."

Inside a bar in House Banfield's domain, there was a great hubbub about all the corrupt officials being purged one after another. Every single one of the bureaucrats who had taken advantage of their positions had been punished for some crime or other.

"Hey, did you hear the lord cut down one of the corrupt officials himself?"

"That's a lie. The kid's like ten, right?"

"It's true! I heard it from a friend of mine who works in a government office!"

"That friend of yours wasn't an official, was he?"

"No, he just cleans the place."

Ever since Liam had taken over, taxes had been going into maintaining facilities within his domain. The size of the military was being reduced, so soldiers were coming back down to the planet's surface to train for new jobs. Rumor had it that their space fleet, which was once thirty thousand ships strong, had been reduced to a tenth of its size.

While noting to himself that he had been getting more customers than usual lately, the bartender chatted with one of his regulars, who was reading an electronic newspaper. There was an article about Liam in it.

"You read this? They're changing compulsory education from three years to six."

"I did," the bartender replied, handing the regular his drink. "Heard they're hurrying to build schools too. A customer in the construction business was laughing about how busy they are."

"Business is booming, eh? It'd be nice if some of that prosperity came my way." The regular was drinking more expensive alcohol than he usually ordered. "This new lord we've got is really something, though, huh? And he's only ten?"

The bartender put a hand on his hip. "It's pretty unbelievable. Five years ago, I never could've guessed this would happen."

Once he'd finished his drink, the customer stared down at his empty glass. "Hope the good news keeps up."

The bartender nodded. "Couldn't agree more."

In his new mansion, Brian was training the freshly hired servants. All the new staff had been selected not just for their looks, but for their skills and character as well. Liam had dismissed anyone who had nothing to offer beyond their appearance.

With serious, hardworking young people before him, Brian felt moved. *We finally have staff who will take their jobs seriously.*

There were quite a few among that staff who seemed rather frightened, however. Liam had recently exposed the wrongdoings of a great deal of corrupt officials, carrying out a massive political purge. All sorts of rumors about the young lord were whizzing around inside his domain. One of these claimed he was quick to anger and would cut down his servants if they displeased him.

Brian attempted to dispel the fears of the new hires. "I'm sure you must be nervous, but Master Liam is very forgiving of those who take their work seriously. There is no need to be afraid of him."

A maid timidly raised her hand.

"Yes?"

"Umm, will Master Liam require, er, nightly duties?"

In this world, it was very much common for the master of a mansion to lay his hands on his workers, common enough that some women sold these services. The female staff were unsettled by the rumors about Liam. They were terrified that if they *did* sell themselves, they'd be killed for even the smallest mistake.

"Master Liam is still young, so you needn't worry about nightly duties. You will likely not even be near him very often, since Amagi takes care of almost all his personal needs."

"He keeps a doll by his side?" someone said.

Brian's eyes narrowed. "I will pretend I did not hear that this time, but there will not be another."

Amagi was a problem that continued to plague Brian. Liam's standing would fall just by keeping her at his side. She was capable, but noble society would never look favorably upon her. After having worked with her for several years, however, Brian could see that Liam trusted her thoroughly. He relied on her almost like a child relies on their mother. Though he was young, Liam was stern and decisive, but even in his apparent maturity, he needed that mother figure. The thought pulled at Brian's heartstrings.

Master Liam is a wise person. He must understand that he was abandoned. Master Cliff, Mistress Darcie, why did you not take more care in raising him?

Brian couldn't bring himself to find fault with the boy. Liam was just trying to fulfill the obligations he'd been saddled with as lord, and Amagi was one of the only figures he could depend on.

"Amagi is very dear to Master Liam. I would suggest not taking a condescending attitude toward her. If Master Liam found out about such a thing, I would not be able to spare you from his wrath."

Though he was young, Liam was already feared by many within his domain. *But things are definitely getting better. With Master Liam, House Banfield will be able to regain its former glory.*

Liam's popularity was rising among his people for purging those corrupt officials. He was building up his reputation as a frightening yet reliable lord. Though he was still young, and his people were still nervous about what the future would hold, they were starting to acknowledge Liam's abilities. Brian believed in him, and he once again pledged his loyalty to his lord in his heart.

I'M THE **EVIL LORD** OF AN **INTERGALACTIC EMPIRE**

4 Liam at Thirty

I N MY PAST LIFE, being thirty years old would have meant a third of your life was behind you. By contrast, thirty-year-olds in this world looked like elementary schoolers and were treated like kids. That part was fine, but there was one problem.

"No good, huh?" I held my sheathed sword in my left hand and looked at the logs around me. Of the three logs I'd placed, I'd at least managed to cut two, but the execution had been rough.

It was a far cry from the special technique Master had shown me. I'd cut far fewer logs, and they were closer to me than they had been to him. I'd spent more than twenty years on this, and still I was only able to achieve a weak imitation. Did I just lack talent?

Master watched me, arms folded and an impassive

expression on his face. Was he disappointed? Becoming nervous, I bowed my head to him and apologized.

"I'm sorry, Master. My skills still pale in comparison to yours."

Master was kind, though, and slowly shook his head. "The path of the sword is a long and arduous one, and there is no prize at the end of it. You've improved much in the last twenty years."

I'd been pondering for all those years how I could achieve what Master had shown me. I couldn't imagine it was something you attained just by practicing the basics. It was then that I recalled another component of the technique Master had mentioned long ago. *Magic.*

"Of course! He used magic. By applying a thin layer of it over the blade, you can extend the sword's reach. Isn't that it?"

Through trial and error, I was eventually able to cut a log that my sword couldn't naturally reach. I hadn't been able to achieve this simply by training my body, and improving my fighting skills hadn't been enough either. My only option had been to use this world's magic.

I thought I had reached the correct answer with this, but my attempts were still very different from Master's technique. Since I wasn't able to pull off the same thing,

I was a little uneasy. But while I fretted that I had failed, Master clapped his hands, impressed.

"You've come so far... You're *incredibly* close. Still, you only get partial credit."

"Partial credit?"

"That's right. If you're going to use magic, then you must study magic."

"But I *am* studying it."

I was a noble, and a count at that, so it was only natural that I'd been studying magic. But in this world, or perhaps just this era, an individual's magical capability wasn't regarded as all that important. Magic wasn't going to protect you against a beam fired from a spaceship. The same principle applied to martial arts. Many nobles still studied them to some degree, but neither martial arts nor magic were a requirement for a noble's station. Rather than learning attack magic and shooting flames from my hand, it would be more efficient to carry a gun.

Not *all* magic was pointless. Healing magic was useful, for instance, and magic was very important in controlling the humanoid weapons of the current era. I would definitely have to learn how to connect with and pilot one of those weapons through the use of magic.

"Yes, well, just learning magic isn't sufficient."

"It isn't?"

I see—just the basics won't be enough. I'll have to get more serious with my studies.

"I'll increase the degree of my magical studies at once."

Master nodded vigorously. Was it just my imagination that he looked a tad nervous? "Very good. You'll have to stop practicing the special technique for a while to make time. Concentrate on magic. Let's see... Ten years should be enough for a start. During that time, I want you to practice only the basics."

And I was making such good progress too! I thought, frustrated, but I couldn't go against my master. If I ever tried to fight him, he would probably chop me to pieces in seconds. I couldn't even picture myself winning, so great was the difference in ability between the two of us.

"I-I understand."

"Very good. In any case, how are things with your domain? You won't be a very good lord if you spend all your time learning martial arts."

How kind my master was to worry about my domain.

"It's fine. My reforms are moving along, and we're finally starting to see real results."

The restructuring of both the military and the government had been going well. I'd decided on expanding some development plans and had started a couple of new projects as well.

Manned construction machines and humanoid robots accomplished their work incredibly quickly. Skyscrapers could be erected in a matter of days. Once, I had seen a structure being built by something like a huge 3D printer. It had rendered me speechless. This disc appeared in the sky, and before I could exclaim "A UFO?!" the disc emitted a light that started to generate a building. People mostly just supplied support, checking the details as the disc did its work. I watched the whole structure being created as though it were a fast-forwarded video—a pretty shocking sight.

If the planet could be so quickly developed, then really, anyone could have done this before. It was a complete mystery to me why my parents and grandparents hadn't. Tax revenue easily increased this way, so there was no reason not to.

"That's good, Liam. Now, how about you show me how you're doing with the basics today?"

"Yes, sir!"

"It wouldn't mean much at this stage to just do so normally, though. From now on, let's blindfold you and add some weights."

"A blindfold and weights, you say?"

Master applied weights to my sword and blindfolded me.

"Swing the sword until it feels as light as a branch in your hands. The blindfold is to teach you that you can't just rely on your eyes."

"Yes, sir!"

I had absolute confidence in my master's training methods, but it was almost like something out of a manga. I had enjoyed reading stuff like that as a kid, but similar entertainment was hard to come by in my domain. That was a rather underdeveloped area, probably because people just didn't have the time or money for such things.

Maybe I should have Amagi make some investments into the entertainment industry too.

Yasushi trembled as he watched a blindfolded Liam swing his weighted sword. His face revealed his emotions, since he knew Liam couldn't see him.

What is this kid? Seriously, what is he?

He had been in a cold sweat ever since Liam had shown him his "special technique." In the past, he'd just casually thought, *Wow, this kid's getting pretty good.* He'd never expected Liam to recreate his parlor tricks as an actual sword technique. Even though he'd only taught the boy the basics, Liam was becoming strong all on his own, and that terrified Yasushi.

After all, Liam had purged every single corrupt official from his domain. He'd been so thorough, it was hard to believe he was still a child. Yasushi had felt detached as he watched all that, thinking, *Ooh, scary.* But if Liam's swordsmanship got any better, things could get very bad for him.

If he finds out I was lying, I'm done for. He'll chop me to pieces in an instant!

Yasushi had merely put on an air of wisdom and fed the boy some pretty words. Liam was already a far better swordsman than him, and if they were to fight, Yasushi could say with absolute confidence that he would lose.

I've got to drag this out to save up some money, then get out of here as soon as I can.

All this time, Yasushi had been lazing around and living a life of relative luxury, burning through his pay as soon as he got it. He'd lied to Liam, telling him he was going off to train when he was actually going into the city to have some fun. He didn't have the funds to make a run for it now.

He wiped the perspiration from his brow as he watched Liam adjust his motions with the blindfold on.

How could he have come so far? Is this kid some kind of genius?

Yasushi was no instructor, and his sword skills were third-rate. He couldn't truly gauge the degree of Liam's talent.

I can't tell. Anyway, I've got to buy some time now. I'll look for more videos for training ideas. If I don't, and he finds out...he'll kill me!

Yasushi had no choice but to stick around despite his fear so he could accrue the funds necessary for his escape. He desperately got to scheming, praying that Liam wouldn't discover his lies.

Is there any reason for the blindfold? I'd wondered at first, but after a while, I caught on to the meaning behind it.

"I understand what you meant now, Master. I'm starting to figure out how to use my other senses. This is what you meant by not relying on my eyes!" I "looked" at Master with the blindfold on. He moved around to get out of my "view," so I followed him with my head.

"Mhm, you mastered that in such a short time," he said, sounding a little surprised. "Really, how did you do this in just a few years?"

He was so baffled by my growth, I could tell he was

cocking his head even with the blindfold on. I spun my weighted sword playfully around my fingers.

"Look, I can swing it so easily now."

"O-oh yeah? No, you can't get conceited!"

"Huh?"

Master was a little harsh when I showed him how confident I was. "It's true that you've honed your other senses, Lord Liam, but that's all you've done—you haven't made them extraordinary yet."

I was surprised to hear this. "So there's even more I can do to avoid relying on my vision?"

"O-of course there is! And that sword is too light for you now, isn't it? I'll prepare a special sword for you."

I felt myself getting excited. "I'm looking forward to it!"

"I-I'm glad."

Huh? Master almost seems scared. Is it just my imagination? Yeah, has to be.

You've gotta be kidding me! Yasushi was terrified when Liam followed his movements with blindfolded eyes, while swinging his weighted sword around like it was nothing. He couldn't just act like a normal person with that blindfold on, now could he? No matter where Yasushi moved, Liam kept turning his face toward him, knowing exactly where he was. He tried to move soundlessly, but it was pointless. All throughout, Liam was smiling—it was creepy.

What to do, what to do?! I didn't think he'd adapt this quickly! Yasushi had tried to buy time with a ridiculous scheme, but it hadn't even taken a few years for Liam to actually learn the skill he only pretended to be teaching him.

Seriously, is he a genius?! If only I'd known he was like this sooner! Yasushi had no way to predict the extent of Liam's potential.

I'll make a super heavy sword and have him use that. That should give him some problems. Yasushi had been talking out of his ass about a sixth sense and supernatural abilities, but he worried that if he kept it up, Liam would truly develop those skills. The thought terrified him.

Hoping to buy some more time, Yasushi came up with a fresh plan. *Oh, I know! That'll be perfect!*

Yasushi made his way to a storehouse on the mansion grounds. This building contained artwork and other items stored during the demolition of the previous mansion. He'd already tried selling off some of the items inside, but they were all fakes.

One of the pieces in the storehouse was an aged humanoid weapon—a mobile knight. It was a large model of the twenty-four-meter class, unlike the fourteen- or eighteen-meter types more popular nowadays, a black behemoth with huge shields mounted on both shoulders. This model was several generations old, probably built hundreds of years ago. It had been used by Liam's great-grandfather, Alistair, and was inferior in every way to modern, mass-produced models.

Yasushi brought Amagi to the storehouse and pointed to the mobile knight. "Make this usable, would you? I'm going to train Liam in it."

Amagi gave him a dubious look. "This model is quite old. Would it not be better to ready a current model for him?"

"We can't do that!"

What worried Yasushi was that the latest mobile knights were extremely easy to pilot. Their specs had improved so much that if someone like Liam—who had loads of time on his hands—got into one, he'd master its controls in a matter of years. Yasushi couldn't buy time if that happened.

"This is for Lord Liam's sake. I'd like you to have it repaired and ready for use."

"These models are no longer in production. Repairing it will take some time. The fourteen- and eighteen-meter models are more commonplace now, so I would recommend using one of those."

Amagi was only treating Yasushi with respect due to Liam's regard for him. If not for that, she would have been far more insistent.

What do I care about your difficulties? I'll make you spend a fortune on it. That much less cash to use later to chase me down.

Yasushi urged Amagi to make use of the old weapon. "Old models are more solidly made. If you give it some upgrades, it'll end up sturdier than the new models."

"It is not that simple. When you balance it out, it is more economical to make use of a current model."

"No, no, no, this one will be better. You should just turn this craft into the ultimate model for Liam's personal use. Don't concern yourselves with the budget."

"There is no logic in using this craft. It is simply a matter of customizing a newer unit for Master's use. It will be cheaper as well."

Yasushi decided to force the issue, since Amagi wouldn't stop arguing with him. "Regardless, I want you to make adjustments to this unit. It will be better for Lord Liam that way. And he should learn to pilot it manually—automatic controls are out of the question! People rely too much on machine assistance these days. There's only meaning in it if you pilot it yourself! He has to use a machine that requires actual skill! Yes, that's for the best!"

All Yasushi wanted was for Liam to use a machine that would be difficult to pilot, but Amagi would never agree with such a thing.

"If the weapon functions well, should he not rely on it?"

"No, he shouldn't! This is something Lord Liam needs to learn!"

At Yasushi's insistence, Amagi had no choice but to oblige. She'd been ordered by Liam to comply with Yasushi's requests as much as possible.

"If you insist, I will hurry and make the arrangements."

"Please. Use as much money as you need. This is for Lord Liam, after all!"

Yasushi piled on all the additions to the mobile knight that he could think of in order to strain their funds.

After Yasushi left the storehouse, Amagi looked up at the mobile knight—personal designation "Avid." Its inner frame showed in places, and parts of its armor had rusted. The interior was even worse, so it couldn't currently be piloted. The machine had been left there to rot.

As she gazed upon the pitiful sight of the Avid, Amagi thought to herself, *Is that man truly a skilled fighter? It's true that Master has gotten stronger, but Yasushi just does not seem terribly impressive to me.* Based on his normal behavior, she couldn't imagine Yasushi was possessed of incredible skill. Still, as long as the man was producing results, there was no real reason to fire him.

No matter how deeply I investigate him, I never find anything suspicious. In fact, his record is almost unnaturally clean. It was almost as if someone had manipulated his record to appear that way.

"I am obligated to carry out his orders. However..." She wasn't sure where to send the Avid for maintenance, but it would have to be a large manufacturer with enough skill to craft the required parts. This was something like taking a classic foreign sports car to a local repair shop; the shop wouldn't have the parts to repair it, and they wouldn't know how to go about performing maintenance either. It made sense to try the original manufacturer.

"This one was manufactured by an Empire factory." The Empire-controlled facility that had made the machine was still in business, so it was likely the best place to send it.

Amagi mulled over Yasushi's requests. "He asked for a great deal. Will we have the funds for all this? In any case, I must proceed." She would have a mechanic examine the Avid and then contact the manufacturer.

She reached out and touched the Avid. She'd rejected Yasushi's suggestions again and again, but there was something almost envious in her expression. "I will do everything I can to restore you, so please protect my master."

When she removed her hand, her face regained its usual neutrality. She left the storehouse, mentally running through the steps necessary to restore the Avid. Along the way, she found Liam walking her way with a blindfold on.

He looked delighted when he noticed her. "Those footsteps must be Amagi."

"You are correct, Master."

Though blindfolded, he had been walking as if he could see where he was going.

"Master, it is dangerous to walk around like that."

"It's fine—it's part of my training. Anyway, I heard you were getting a mobile knight ready for me?"

Amagi told him about the requests Yasushi had made for the mobile knight.

"He would like an old model to be repaired for use, even though a newer one would be more within our budget."

Bringing a hand to his chin, Liam cocked his head. "My master must have his reasons. Anyway, I'll leave it to you. I'm gonna take a walk around the mansion."

Liam left with the blindfold still on, but Amagi was concerned that he would fall, so she followed along behind him.

The bar in House Banfield's domain was thriving again today.

"Cheers!"

A group of men who had stopped in on their way home from work were drinking and laughing. There were still occasional fights here, but it was a far cry from thirty years ago. The seats were fuller than they were empty now, and the bartender fondly watched the staff he'd had to hire as they hurried about their tasks.

One of his regulars called out, "Looks like business is booming, barkeep."

"Hm? Yeah, I was finally able to hire some help."

Unlike before, when he had only been able to sell cheap liquor, there was some pretty expensive booze flying off his shelves these days. The regular who'd spoken was also dressed better than he used to be, and the drink he sipped was higher quality than his old swill. He previously seemed to want to drown himself in booze, but now he could savor the finer stuff.

The bartender pivoted the conversation. "By the way, how's work?"

"It's great. Too great, really. I'm too busy." The regular, who had previously complained about not having any work, was now griping about having too much. His expression was cheery, though, as if he felt truly fulfilled. "Hard to believe things could change so much just because we got a new lord," he mused, reflecting on the past.

The bartender readied another drink for him and responded, "If my grandpa's to be believed, things were even better in his time."

"How many hundreds of years ago was this?"

"Four or five?"

"Strange how things were more developed back then."

House Banfield's domain was starting to win back some of that former vitality.

"The lord's being pretty quiet lately, though. Haven't heard a thing about him in the last twenty years."

No one had heard a peep from Liam since his big political purge two decades ago. There were rumors, of course, but all of them lacked credibility.

The bartender was curious too. "I've heard he really likes dolls, but it's hard to hold it against him when he's doing such a good job."

"I thought all nobles hated dolls. Guess this lord's different."

"Can't say I care either way. As long as business is this good, I couldn't be happier."

The regular bought the bartender a drink, and the two of them made a toast to their future prosperity.

5 The Avid

WHEN I REACHED my mid-thirties, the mobile knight my great-grandfather had used was returned to us, fully repaired. It was a humanoid weapon with an extra pair of arms holding huge shields at both shoulders, otherwise covered in knight-like armor. I'd previously thought the humanoid design made no sense, but in this world, it seemed easier to maneuver huge weapons if they were in human shape since magic was employed in their operation.

Fantasy worlds sure are crazy.

In the storehouse, I gazed up at the Avid and thought the thing really made an impression. Before, it had just been an immobile decoration, but now it practically sparkled like new.

"This is amazing. I'd heard it was old too; you did a great job repairing it."

Beside me stood an engineer officer of the Empire's Seventh Weapons Factory. She wore orange coveralls and had an ID card pinned at her left breast, with glasses and dark hair that fell to her shoulders. This beautiful girl with an intellectual look was the engineering lieutenant. Her name was Nias Carlin.

She explained to me with a smile, "It was a pretty tough job, to be honest. I never thought I'd be repairing this unit."

"You were familiar with it?"

"Well, it was a model developed by our factory—there's one just like it in our filing vault. Our most experienced techs said it was like going back to the old days."

Extra-large units like these weren't common these days, but I figured too big was better than too small. As I admired the Avid, satisfied, Nias shot me a troubled look.

"Is this really going to be all right, though? All the assist functions were removed, so I think it'll be pretty difficult to pilot."

Is it like the difference between a manual and an automatic car?

Nias seemed to want to add assist functions to the Avid to lessen the burden of piloting it. My master, who was also standing there with us, crossed his arms and smiled.

"There's no need to worry—Lord Liam will master this in no time. But I'd like to go over some of the details of the craft, so if you could come to my room..."

Master reached out to Nias's shoulder, but she dodged him with a grin. "It's all in the manual, no need to worry. And it's the count who'll be piloting it, right? If I'm going to give anyone pointers, it should be Lord Liam, shouldn't it?"

"I-I guess you're right."

Master's shoulders slumped at this rejection. I guessed Nias was his type. For a moment, I thought maybe I should order her to spend some time with him, as an evil lord would, but I quickly discarded the idea. Master was a skilled swordsman; if he'd been serious, Nias wouldn't have been able to dodge him. The fact that she had obviously meant that he had let her go, so he'd probably only been joking.

Anyway, Master was probably too upstanding to appreciate a gift like that. Plus, Nias was an Imperial officer, not merely one of my subjects, so that made me hesitant to lay a finger on her. Also, it probably wouldn't be wise to get on the bad side of the person performing maintenance on my craft. If something ever went wrong with the unit, I'd be in trouble.

"Let's get into the cockpit. I'll join you, if you don't mind, so I can explain how to operate it."

Guided by Nias, I headed for the cockpit with a smile. Piloting a humanoid weapon... I'd been greatly looking forward to this moment.

The Avid stood outside the storehouse now, some distance from the mansion. I'd been expecting the cockpit to be cramped, but it was a lot more spacious than I'd anticipated.

"It's pretty big in here."

"This cockpit was expanded using special magic. Its seat is made of the highest-quality materials for maximum comfort as well. There are no assist functions, but other than that, every aspect of the unit is top-class."

I sat down in the cushioned seat. It felt almost as though it wrapped around my body, the way it supported me—and just as I thought that, it actually *did* wrap itself around my body. The seat moved and restructured itself to match my form. The control sticks moved automatically to where my hands were, positioned perfectly for my access.

"Very nice. Looks good too—the black armor is badass."

"Guys really like black, huh? There are a lot of black units."

To nobles, mobile knights were a symbol of military power. Many of them owned personal units for this reason, and because they just looked cool. They even used them for decorations, decking them out as they pleased.

"It's rare for people to spend so much money fixing up one unit, though."

"Is it? I hear some people make them super flashy."

That was why Master had said we should spend as much money as needed. To compare it to something from my last life, it was like owning a car. *Well, if anything, a battleship is probably closer to a car than this.* Anyway, mobile knights were a status symbol for nobles.

"Well, a lot of them are mass-produced units that have simply been modified, but since we had such a sizable budget, our engineers really went all out. Everyone had a lot of fun since it's rare for a noble to care more about the inside of a unit than the outside. Now, why don't you start the engine?"

One switch fired up the engine, and the craft began a scan of my body. It confirmed me as its pilot and set itself to prevent being piloted by anyone else.

"You're designated as the pilot now, my lord; this unit won't move for anyone but you. It's your own personal craft."

"That's got a nice ring to it."

I gripped the control sticks and moved them, and the view around me...changed. The cockpit only shook a little, though.

"H-huh?" The Avid was now lying on the ground, but artificial gravity kept me feeling correctly oriented. It was a strange sensation.

Nias had a look on her face that said, *Thought so.*

"All the assist functions, like the auto balancer, have been removed from this machine. That means it'll be a lot more difficult to control. If you master it, though, you'll be able to move it just like your own body."

I caught on to what Master wanted for me.

"If I can master this, then I'll be on my way to becoming a top-notch pilot."

"I'd say if you can *use* this thing, you'll already be a top-notch pilot. But if you can't control it, you'll lose to any mass-produced model. If you do master it, it's possible you could be stronger than any other unit out there—depending on the pilot, anyway."

"Perfect!"

I gripped the control sticks and concentrated. I had to start by standing up. Unlike a video game where you could just enter simple commands, to stand in this machine, you had to move the unit's arms and legs simultaneously. Each individual motion had to be controlled manually, which was incredibly difficult to do, and this was why they used magic in the process. In fact, you could say that was the main reason people learned magic. With magic, you could visualize the delicate movements of a human body and transmit that imagery to the machine. That was why humanoid weapons were easier for the people of this world to use than they would've been otherwise. With non-humanoid weapons, it was harder for the user to envision the movements, which would in turn confuse the machines.

The Avid slowly stood, and Nias was impressed.

"You're very good for a first-timer."

"Of course I am—I've practiced in a simulator."

"That's not what I mean. This unit's much harder to control than a regular mobile knight. If you're doing this well on your first try, my lord, you've got a real knack for it."

"And you're a real flatterer."

"It's not flattery," Nias said with a slight frown.

Meanwhile, I concentrated as hard as I could on moving the Avid. It slowly raised one leg and took a step forward. That movement alone was incredibly complex. I was beginning to worry whether I'd even be able to walk in this thing. I started breathing heavier from the effort, and Nias placed her hands atop mine on the controls.

She leaned forward, and I experienced the gentle scent and warmth of a woman.

"It's very important to maintain a strong mental image to control this unit. You'll have to concentrate on your magic the whole time. Now, move the control sticks slowly. It'll be easier if you think of the whole craft as your own body."

I moved the craft slowly at first, one step at a time, gradually upping the pace. One wrong move could send it tumbling to the ground again. Nias was giving me a rundown on the Avid, so I listened to her as I focused on moving.

"This baby's real strong and sturdy. Your average unit won't be a match for it, but that makes it all the more difficult to maneuver. Keep that in mind. He'll be tough to master."

Nias was so concentrated on her explanation that she got a little too close to me. One of her breasts touched my shoulder, and I suddenly found all my attention drawn to that spot.

"Also, here—"

I focused on Nias, and the Avid came to a halt. Her body was toned, as if she worked out, but had fat in all the right places. I hadn't noticed before due to her coveralls, but she had a pretty good figure. All my attention was on her chest where it pressed against me.

Then, sensing my thoughts or in tune with my magic, the Avid started moving its hands without my conscious command.

"Oh? What's wrong? You should start from walk—wait!"

Nias figured out what the movements meant and pulled away from me, covering her chest with her arms. Her cheeks had flushed red.

"N-no! That's not what I—"

The Avid was moving its hands as though it were groping a woman's breasts.

"Let's take a break. Huh? Communications are cut off. Is that a mistake with the settings?"

Brian watched the Avid from afar. It was as if the mobile knight of Lord Alistair, whom he had respected so much, had come alive again. The sight moved him. Its parts might have been different, but it was still Alistair's Avid.

"Lord Alistair... Lord Liam is piloting your unit. It moves me to te—huh?"

His tears dried when the Avid, the craft of the honorable Alistair, started making improper movements with its hands.

"Lord Liam, *what* in the world are you doing?"

Inside, he already knew. The officer who'd accompanied the Avid here was an attractive woman, and they were alone together in the cockpit. He'd worried the moment he saw her that Liam would try putting his hands on her, as he'd always been quite physical with Amagi. Though, he'd also worried that maybe Liam didn't have an interest in anything other than dolls; he had never pursued a living woman before. Now that his interest in real women had been made clear, Brian was relieved for multiple reasons, one of which being the question of whether Liam would ever produce an heir.

However, Brian couldn't condone the hand movements the mobile knight was making. The thought that the beloved craft of his Lord Alistair was gesturing in such a shameful way almost brought him to tears of another kind.

To see Master Alistair's craft making such lewd movements... I just can't bear it.

The Avid was replicating detailed motions with its fingers, as if there were breasts in its grasp. *At least cut the power before you do that!* Brian thought, but he had no choice but to watch from a safe distance. There was no telling when the craft might topple to the ground. To make matters worse, communications were shut off, as Liam wasn't responding to any outside calls.

Was this his plan from the start?

While Brian agonized, Yasushi was making a racket, a blue vein popping out on his forehead. "That brat's groping the lieutenant's tits! Are they soft? Huh?!"

The machine's fingertips made a motion as if they were pinching something, and Yasushi reached a tipping point, frantically calling out to Liam over and over again.

"Lord Liam, get out of there right now! You can't do something so exciting—er, so disgraceful in the cockpit! Get down here! Lord Liam? Can you hear me?"

Yasushi played his part when in Liam's presence, but as soon as the count was out of sight, his attitude changed dramatically. Like Amagi, Brian didn't trust him.

How is Master Liam showing such impressive results when he's learning from a man like this? With Liam making such progress, they couldn't just kick Yasushi out, and every time Brian reported the man's poor behavior, Liam just wrote it off out of respect for his master. Eventually Brian had decided to just keep quiet. Yasushi wasn't doing any actual harm, and Liam *was* constantly improving. Brian even felt somewhat indebted to the man for having Amagi restore the Avid. With her preference for efficiency, she would never have done it otherwise.

"Get down here, you stupid brat!" Yasushi shouted.

Amagi narrowed her eyes at him, and he hastily apologized.

"Oh, sorry about that. I just got a little emotional." He offered an obsequious bow to the doll, sweat beading his forehead.

Is this man really *a master swordsman and martial artist?* Brian couldn't help wondering.

I'm never forgiving that bastard! Yasushi was enraged at his apprentice for putting his hands on Nias, whom he desired himself. He was too afraid to actually scold Liam and make him angry, however, so he decided to get back at him by making his training even more grueling. A man of small character—that was Yasushi.

The revenge he came up with was harsher training than Liam had ever experienced.

"You're beginning to tremble, Lord Liam." Arms crossed, Yasushi glared at the sweating Liam.

"I-I'll try harder." Blindfolded, Liam stood atop an unstable log, holding an extremely heavy sword. He'd already been made to undergo several other acts, such as walking a tightrope like some street performer. Yasushi forced upon Liam whatever harsh training he could think of to get back at him.

"What are you going to do when you have to wield your sword on unstable footing? Now, again."

Liam was sweating, exhausted. If Yasushi pushed him *too* hard, to the point of injury, it would be all over for him, so he did his best to gauge Liam's limits and dole out punishment accordingly.

"Once you're finished with this, it's back to pilot training. No time for rest."

"Understood, Master!"

Liam listened well and worked hard, but he'd put his hands on a woman Yasushi had wanted for himself, and the man just couldn't get past it.

Now that it's come to this, I'm gonna keep demanding harder and harder training. I'm gonna give you one trial after another that even you can't handle, and it'll grind that pride of yours into dust! You'll lose all your confidence, kid!

Nias stayed on for three months, leaving only when she'd finished instructing them on maintenance and explaining the ins and outs of the craft. She would return eventually, and Yasushi vowed to get her contact information when she did.

"Your legs are shaking, Lord Liam. You haven't trained enough!"

"I-I'll redouble my efforts."

"Of course you will. Starting today, we're going to pick up the pace."

And so, Yasushi trained Liam much, much harder out of a personal grudge.

I'll make your training impossible and break you! So Yasushi thought as he devised all sorts of new training methods.

"Drop deaaad!"

He had set up pitching machines that shot rubber balls at a blindfolded Liam from every angle. They were only rubber balls, so they wouldn't seriously injure him, but they still hurt when they hit him.

"Ack!"

"What's wrong, Lord Liam? If you can't handle this, you'll never be able to call yourself a warrior!" Yasushi cackled. Feeling victorious, he held up the device that controlled the machines assaulting Liam.

See that, brat? That's 'cause you got too full of yourself!

There was no way for Liam to evade the rubber balls with the blindfold on.

No matter how strong you are, there's nothin' you can do

against this. Yasushi smirked and increased the speed at which the balls were fired.

"You must use your mind's eye, Lord Liam. Rely on your sixth...uh, your seventh sense and swing your sword." He spouted some bullshit, giving Liam the impression that he was doing all this for his sake. All he had to do was come up with lines like this and Liam would believe anything he said.

"No! Swing your sword, Lord Liam!"

"B-but, Master, I only have one sword! I can't deal with this many of them!"

An ugly smile spread on Yasushi's face. "Nothing is impossible in this world, Lord Liam! Now, find the answer for yourself!"

There was no way he could hit the balls; what Yasushi demanded was impossible. Nevertheless, a change occurred within Liam at that moment. The combination of his vastly overdone basic training and all the ridiculous training methods that Yasushi had sourced from free videos produced an unexpected result.

Liam held the sword out in front of him, and several rubber balls moved in a strange way, as though they were being knocked away before they struck him. At first, Yasushi dismissed it, thinking he was mistaken, but the number of deflected balls gradually increased.

"Huh?" His jaw dropped. It was as if there were a barrier around Liam. Eventually, no matter how many rubber balls he fired at Liam, none of them connected.

Still blindfolded, Liam smiled. "So this is what you meant, Master! I finally understand!"

You...understand? Huh? Understand what?

Liam relaxed his posture, but the rubber balls still failed to strike him. In fact, the range of the barrier only increased.

"A wall of magic. You meant for me to protect myself like this, right?"

What is he saying? Can you really just conjure a force field like that? I've never heard of it before! Is this kid a master magician too?!

Liam had manifested a magical barrier around himself, but that wasn't the end of it.

"Once you understand it, it's simple: the Way of the Flash is a mixed style of swordsmanship *and* magic. So..."

Liam swung his sword to create a spiral of air that whipped all the balls upward as though they were caught in a tornado. Just when Liam could no longer be seen behind the whirlwind, it suddenly disappeared.

"Gah!" In the next instant, one of the rubber balls flew into Yasushi's wide-open mouth.

Huh? What? What just happened? He looked around

and found the pitching devices plugged with rubber balls. Yasushi let the ball drop from his mouth, and when it hit the ground, it split in two. All the other balls on the ground were split in a similar way.

Freed from the rain of rubber balls, Liam walked over to Yasushi and faced him even with the blindfold on, smiling. The sight terrified Yasushi.

"Well, Master? Did I have the right idea?"

Yasushi trembled like a newborn fawn, his thoughts racing. *What the hell? I don't get it. How did he become so strong just from the basics and whatever scams I came up with? Is he genuinely a genius?* Yasushi hadn't realized that all along he'd been training a complete monster. *This is too much. I don't want to be involved with him anymore.*

He did his best to play his part. "Wonderful, Lord Liam. Now there is nothing more I can teach you."

"Master?"

Yasushi continued his act even as a cold sweat ran down his brow, relieved that Liam was wearing the blindfold. "You have only the secret technique yet to master, but I'm sure you'll manage on your own, Lord Liam. I leave you to pursue whatever training you desire from here on. The only thing I have left to teach you is that there is no end to the path of true swordsmanship. You must simply remain diligent."

He tried to wrap things up neatly, but Liam interjected, "I-I don't want that! I want you to train me more, Master! I'll even open up a dojo just for you, here in my domain!"

If you do that, I won't be able to get away!

Yasushi turned him down gently. "I'm honored by your offer, but I have not yet finished my own journey. It is too soon for me to open up a dojo."

"Master... Th-then at least gauge my skill. I just want to know how far along my secret technique is."

"Of course, I don't mind."

Liam removed his blindfold. "I'll ready the logs, then."

"There's no need to do it just this second."

Yasushi wiped the sweat from his brow as he watched Liam run off to fetch some logs. "I-I gotta get outta here. If he ever finds out I'm a fake, he'll kill me. I won't even be able to defend myself."

He made plans to award Liam as a full master of his sword style and then get the hell off the planet.

A door between worlds opened, and the Guide stepped through. He stood atop the mansion's roof and searched for Liam, feeling excited.

"Now, how is little Liam doing? Oh? His domain seems to have advanced quite a bit." Apparently, Liam was doing better than the Guide had anticipated, but this didn't bother him too much, considering it would make his eventual fall from grace all the sweeter.

"And what about that swindler—is he doing his job?" Whether the fake had been found out by Liam and cut down or was still deceiving him, it didn't matter. Either way, the Guide was sure to be entertained.

At last, the Guide spotted Liam in the mansion's courtyard. He had logs lined up all around him, but they were too far away for his sword to reach.

"Oh, he's training? I look forward to seeing how his skill has developed."

As Liam had lived a sheltered life, learning swordsmanship from a swindler, the Guide couldn't imagine he had anywhere near the skill level of an average knight in this world. If he was satisfied with his meager skill, it would be amusing.

There was a significant gap in the ability levels between individuals in this world. It made quite a difference whether a person regularly spent time in an education capsule in childhood or just used it once or twice and didn't let the education really stick after that. This was a world where those born with talent were seldom given the opportunity to make use of it to get ahead. Only those who received a solid education—nobles and knights, mainly—were able to become strong.

Knights were a special sort. With their swordsmanship, they could even defeat soldiers armed with guns. The Guide thought that Liam, who'd been educated by a charlatan, would be nothing but a pale imitation, a mockery of someone with actual skill. Once he went out into the real world, he would learn how powerless he was and become heartbroken.

However, though the frog in the well knows nothing of the vast ocean, the one thing it knows perfectly is the beauty of the sky.

Liam pushed up the guard of his sword with his left thumb, then let it fall back with a *clink*.

"Oh? What is he—huh?" All the Guide could do in response to the sight unfolding before him was let out a dumbfounded "Wha—?!"

All the logs around Liam fell to the ground, cut by a sword that had moved faster than the eye could see.

"Wait, that's—you can't be serious!" The Guide couldn't believe what he was seeing. During the thirty years that he'd left Liam alone, he had become incredibly strong.

The doll and the butler who were watching Liam applauded.

"Well done, Master."

"Very impressive, Master Liam."

It was a mind-boggling sight. Even with magic and a superior physique, there were only a handful of people in this world who could reach this level. Amagi handed Liam a towel, which he used to wipe away his sweat.

"I still haven't reached my master's level. I wanted to learn more from him, but he just disappeared after awarding me full mastery." Though he was already a first-rate swordsman, he didn't let it go to his head and showed no sign of being content with his skill.

The Guide was overcome with bewilderment. *What did that man do? How did this happen?* He quickly called up a screen to search for Yasushi and located him drinking at a tavern on whatever planet he'd fled to.

A woman sat beside him at the bar, keeping him company.

"What is that kid? I just don't get it."

"Are you talking about your apprentice again, Mr. Yasushi?"

Yasushi griped, *"I'm a second-rate swordsman... no, third-rate. But no matter how stupid my ideas were, that kid actually found a way to put them into practice. In ten years, he'd surpassed me, and in twenty years, he was just a step away from being first-rate."*

The woman laughed, apparently finding this funny. *"And in the last ten years, you made him a first-rate swordsman, huh? Your jokes are so funny, Mr. Yasushi."*

She didn't believe him, but Yasushi insisted that he wasn't joking. *"It's true! In the end, the kid even said he wanted to build a proper dojo for me so I could teach swordsmanship there. I got so scared, I had to run. There's something wrong with that kid. I mean, who the hell can cut their opponent without even drawing their sword? It's crazy!"*

Yasushi couldn't believe that Liam had recreated the street magician act he'd showed him as an actual sword technique. The Guide banished the image and put a hand to his forehead. He had a headache, and it was all because of Liam. He could sense Liam's feelings of gratitude and heard his thoughts as though they were spoken.

I've really been blessed, the boy was thinking. *I was able to learn swordsmanship from such a great teacher, and development in my domain has come so far from where it was when I took over as lord. At first, I almost thought I'd been tricked, but that Guide was the real deal. What an incredible guy.*

The feelings of gratitude the Guide had intercepted sickened him. It was negative emotions he craved, and this sort of goodwill made him nauseated. Liam's thankfulness was so strong that it was unpleasant for the Guide to even be in this world.

"I guess I have some thinking to do."

The Guide knew he had to come up with a way to cause Liam suffering instead.

6 Honey Trap

MISERABLE FROM the thankfulness Liam was sending his way, the Guide thought hard about how to fill him with hatred, resentment, and disgust.

"I need to make him unhappy, but the only people he has in his life are the old butler and the doll. There's no way for me to deal him any emotional damage. If there were a human woman in the picture, I'd be able to dredge up some of the trauma from his old life, but..."

He thought about having someone who worked for Liam stir up some kind of trouble, but all the government officials who might have made mischief had been executed, so that was out. He needed to find some sort of pawn...

If he had to, he could create one, but it would spoil the fun to interfere so directly. It wasn't to his taste to orchestrate everything himself. The Guide's typical strategy was to generate some small impetus and watch how events played out after that. At the same time, he wanted to straighten out this Liam business quickly, so he was having a tough time deciding.

"I thought he'd have dozens of women serving him and be doing whatever he desired, but he's been surprisingly diligent."

Liam had supposedly planned on becoming an evil lord, but he was governing his people like a benevolent ruler. *Did he forget his own goal, or what?* the Guide wondered.

When Liam was alone in his office, he finally stretched and smirked.

"Oh?" When the Guide read his thoughts, he found that Liam had his own ideas on how to be an evil lord.

My domain's flourishing now, and my people have more economic freedom. It really is a good thing I helped them attain some wealth before squeezing them dry. I mean, what was I supposed to do with their dregs?

The Guide was pleased to find that Liam hadn't forgotten his goal, after all. If he'd had a change of heart, the Guide might have just crushed him between his fingers right then and there.

"I see—just like me, he intends to raise them up before knocking them down. Certainly not a bad idea.

That means I can expect interesting developments in the future."

Liam mulled over his future plans. *Should I start by collecting a beautiful harem? Considering my domain's population, there's gotta be at least one or two peerless beauties around here.*

The Guide became giddy listening to Liam contemplate gathering up women against their will. "Wonderful. Now I can see just how vulgar and narrow-minded you are. Whether you kidnap them or buy them, you'll never own their hearts. Oh, that gets me every time. Ahh, but maybe I'll let them whisper sweet nothings to each other, then introduce another man to steal her away from him. I'm sure Liam would just love that!"

Just then Amagi entered the room to spoil the Guide's fun. He clicked his tongue and watched the exchange with resentment.

"You want to transfer personnel from the military?"

"Yes. We would be taking on reserve soldiers and those close to retirement. I had inquired about purchasing unused surplus from the army, and they asked if we desire personnel as well."

The Guide decided he could make use of the Imperial Army's suggestion. "Hmm. The army probably wants to get rid of some of their problematic members."

The army seemed to want to demote some of its soldiers and sweep them out to the boonies, leaving them for this backwater lord to deal with. Like the Guide, Liam caught on to this and frowned. *"They're just going to send us useless people, aren't they?"*

"They will send us Imperial soldiers, some of them perhaps graduates of the Imperial Military Academy. They will be well educated and professionally trained, with experience in real combat. I believe such personnel are necessary to strengthen our private armada."

Amagi's words were persuasive, and Liam was forced to agree.

The Guide's lips twisted into a smile. "I have the perfect idea to sow a few seeds for the future. I'll make sure he gets a nice contingent of earnest warriors who would never stand for an evil lord, then wait for them to rebel against him. This is looking to be quite fun after all."

Liam had been working hard to ensure that he could torment his people as an evil lord at a later stage. He surely wouldn't appreciate soldiers of good moral character who would stand with the people when they staged an uprising and strung Liam up. A warmth spread through the Guide as he imagined Liam's own men executing him.

"Now, let me go make sure the men who get sent to him are nice and upstanding. I spare no effort when it comes to follow-ups, do I? Sometimes I even think I work too much!"

The Guide snapped his fingers and black smoke spewed from his body, dispersing into the air around him. He tilted his hat down low and stepped through the door between worlds.

"Really, though, there's nothing more nauseating than gratitude. I feel sick just being here. Best to spend some time elsewhere for a while. Please entertain me when next I arrive, little Liam."

A fleet of old-style battleships had arrived at House Banfield's domain. Commanding them was a brigadier general of the Imperial Army, an elite who had graduated with top marks from the military academy and steadily risen in rank. However, his rise had ended when he exposed the wrongdoings of the noble who was his commanding officer. While his contemporaries continued their career paths, he alone remained a brigadier general, relegated to a fleet that merely patrolled a remote region. The fleet was notorious for being staffed by the army's undesirables, cruising an area that would never see combat with an enemy force.

There were in fact several such fleets, and due to the whims of some higher-up or other, it had been decided a few of them should be disposed of. They'd found a noble who wanted to acquire the aged battleships, and the people manning them were part of the package.

"So the army's selling people now too. It's rotten to the core," the brigadier general muttered on his bridge, but no one around him was listening. The personnel he'd been given for this reassignment was a collection of strong-willed troublemakers who had butted heads with their superiors, a good number of whom had been demoted for defying a noble.

"What a bunch of misfits."

One of the operators on the bridge informed him that they were nearing the planet of House Banfield.

"We're receiving a communication from House Banfield, General."

"Patch them through."

The general thought poorly of nobles' private armies, and he lamented the fact that now he was going to belong to one of them. However, as a man who'd spent many years in the military, he knew of no other way to live. He couldn't just choose another path at this point in his life.

A bunch of misfits, including me. Well, I wonder what this noble who bought us will be like.

What sort of things would they be forced to do for House Banfield? Many of his soldiers worried about the answer to that question, and as the man leading them, the brigadier general puffed out his chest, determined to make a strong impression.

I was now in my mid-forties. Would I have considered myself old at this point in my past life? Maybe not quite yet. In *this* world, I was just now approaching adulthood. As for my life, it was just more of the same. I was still overseeing my domain, studying, and training my body. Why? Call it the preparation phase of my evil deeds. Actually, I felt like I had been doing quite well, so I didn't see a problem with just continuing on in this way.

As I was finishing up some work in my office, Amagi arrived with a report. "Master, Engineering Lieutenant Nias Carlin of the Seventh Weapons Factory is requesting to meet with you. She wishes to inquire as to the status of the Avid."

"Nias?" *So that beautiful engineering lieutenant has finally returned to my territory.* "She came all the way here just to see the Avid?"

"Checking on the status of the Avid is likely just a pretext. I believe her true intention is to peddle the wares of the Seventh Weapons Factory."

The Empire had a lot of rough edges, which was understandable for an intergalactic organization. Its immense scale meant that countless issues ended up being treated as trivial matters. For instance, any old noble could buy armaments from an Empire-managed weapons factory. There were terms for buying and selling such things, but they were lax, hence the factory rep who'd come here acting like a door-to-door salesman.

"Guess she figures our finances are good enough now for us to afford her products. Brand-new battleships are gonna be expensive though, huh?"

I supposed it would be comparable to buying a used car versus a new car. Most of House Banfield's current military vessels were a generation old. In order to cut costs, our main force was far from top-grade, but I considered our ships plenty adequate. Right now, I didn't have any gripes.

"She should offer her stuff to the Imperial Army or to richer nobles, instead of trying to sell it to me."

"I took the liberty of looking into the reputation of the Seventh Weapons Factory, and while they seem to be recognized for high-quality manufacturing, they are also known for inferior design. The consistent quality also makes their prices high. All things considered, they have a middling reputation within the Empire. The Third Weapons Factory is much more highly regarded and excels in both quality and design."

Nias's factory being the seventh meant that there were obviously more weapons factories in the Empire. I imagined things were hard for them with so much competition, but that had nothing to do with me, so I couldn't say I much cared one way or the other.

I replied to Amagi in the affirmative regarding Nias's request, then headed to my reception room.

Upon my arrival to the reception room, I found Nias there waiting for me. She was in her military uniform today instead of her work clothes, though the tight skirt she wore looked awfully short to me. Noticing my gaze, Amagi whispered to me, "That uniform breaches Imperial Army regulations."

When I sat down on the couch, I understood what she meant. Nias had on some pretty daring underwear.

After we greeted each other, Nias attempted to make small talk rather than launch right into her sales pitch. "You've grown a lot, my lord. I hardly recognized you."

"Right. So what did you want to say?" She had probably meant to compliment me, but I didn't feel that I'd grown all that much. To me it was just lip service, a stock phrase you'd say to a kid.

"I thought I would come and see how the Avid is doing. How's it been lately?"

I let my gaze flick down to the gap between her thighs, peering inside her skirt. "That's not what you're here for. You've got something to sell me, don't you?"

My domain was much more developed now, and I was generating a lot more tax money. When they caught a whiff of my newly improved financial situation, all sorts of people showed up to sell me things. Nias was one of them.

She took out a tablet and fiddled with it, producing some 3D images that appeared in front of me. "Right to the point, eh? I appreciate that. Would you like to purchase any of the ships or weapons from the Seventh Factory?"

The images that hovered before me were small, but they had quite a bit of impact. The holograms were incredibly realistic, almost like elaborate miniatures floating around me, and underneath each image was an absurd figure—the price.

Yeah, new cars—I mean, new ships are pricey.

"They're much more expensive than the ships we're using."

"Well, vessels like this have grades to them, you see. They'll cost substantially more than ships with only the bare minimum of capabilities."

For the price of one new high-powered battleship, I could buy three used lower-grade ships.

Amagi perused the images and added some information that Nias hadn't provided. "You will also have to pay tax on anything you buy from an Empire-owned weapons factory. These prices are before tax."

I glanced at Nias to find her averting her gaze, a nervous smile on her face. "I-I can guarantee a high level of performance, though! The latest models have multiple improvements, far surpassing previous ships in several areas! Take this cruiser, for example—it can accommodate many more mobile knights than previous models. It performs much better as a fighting ship as well!"

In other words, they've made some minor improvements to previous models, so she's here to push them on me. Sure, they've got great functionality, but what do you want me to do with 'em?

"Sell 'em to the Imperial Army."

Looking glum, Nias covered her face with both hands. "They weren't picked up in preliminary trials."

The Empire tended to do things in broad strokes, so each fleet in the Imperial Army could choose the factory it bought its ships from. For this reason, trial ones were constantly being held. Nias had just revealed that the Seventh Weapons Factory hadn't sold any of its ships following their trial runs.

Amagi coolly presented the results of her analysis. "In this instance, the problem does not lie with the performance."

Nias made excuses, almost sounding like she was about to cry. "Our vessels were superior in a number of ways, but they kept saying things like 'They're smaller than the previous models,' 'I don't like the design,' or 'The interior looks cheap'!"

As a matter of status, nobles prioritized outward appearance and interior design. There were some commoners who'd reached the upper brass of the military, but nobles made up an overwhelming majority. If there wasn't a huge difference in the specs between two ships, they'd obviously go with the model that looked more impressive. In their place, I would choose the one with the better design myself.

There were people who prioritized functionality, but when you compared two military vessels of the same type, there wasn't much of a difference. If I was right and Nias's factory had only made minor improvements to their previous models, resulting in a disappointing design and price-performance ratio, there was no incentive to buy their new ones.

"Wh-what do you say, my lord? How about just two hundred ships. No, make it one hundred! You won't even have to pay for them all up front! Could you please think it over?"

I figured the Seventh Weapons Factory hadn't anticipated doing so poorly in their trials. They'd probably only come to me because of their mountain of overstock.

"Can you display ships from other factories, Amagi?"

"Of course."

Small 3D images of battleships from other weapons factories popped up around Amagi. When I looked at the other ships, I realized that the ones from the Seventh Factory had a bluntness about them. Perhaps even "bluntness" was an understatement. They were all function and no form, practically screaming, "We're weapons!" I just couldn't warm up to them. Ships from other factories with the same basic structure boasted much more refined designs. I understood why the Seventh Factory's ships weren't successful. There was no way for them to compete.

When I compared all the different ships Amagi previewed, the ones from the Third Weapons Factory looked especially cool. Those would sell for sure.

"This one's good, isn't it, Amagi? Let's make this one my flagship."

"You would need permission from the Empire to purchase a vessel of the flagship class, Master. I fear that it would not be granted to House Banfield."

Looks like I can't buy anything over two thousand meters. I'll have to stick to the thousand-meter ships, then. But is a thousand meters considered small? How can I judge?

"Oh yeah? That's too bad."

It turned out that the reason I couldn't buy such a craft was because up until recently, House Banfield had been behind on the taxes it owed the Empire. The payments were finally getting made, but the damage had been done, and the Empire was still treating me coldly. I guessed that if I asked them for permission to acquire a flagship, they'd demand I first get all of House Banfield's back taxes up to date. I didn't think it made sense for me as an evil lord to be dutifully paying taxes, but nothing good would come from standing up to my superiors. If you can't beat 'em, pay 'em. *Doing evil on my home turf and sucking up to the Empire... I'm a two-bit villain. Well, it is what it is.*

"Guess I'll settle for this type, then. It looks cooler than what I've got right now, anyway." I indicated an eight-hundred-meter class craft, though it was a little small.

"I will contact the Third Weapons Factory, then."

We were having this conversation right in front of Nias, and she cut in. "Wait a second! We're really in trouble here!"

I realized that, but it wasn't as if it were my fault. "Well, your designs suck."

"But isn't functionality more important? You can't see the outside of a ship when you're in one!"

"If the specs aren't that different, then you have to choose based on design, don't you? But the inside's a problem too. 'Looks cheap' doesn't cover it. When there's this little effort invested, it just seems like you're doing it out of spite."

I opened up the interior of one of the Seventh Factory holograms. The passageways were so narrow, it was as if the designer had been purposely trying to inconvenience the buyer. It didn't even seem like they'd accounted for the crew. There was only so far you could go to reduce wastefulness.

"Our productivity and serviceability are in a different league from the other factories!"

"That's not the problem."

"Th-then..." Refusing to back down, Nias swiftly removed her jacket. Through her white blouse, I could make out a pretty flashy bra. Was this the sort of thing one wore when they wanted to make a statement? As I watched her push her breasts together in an enticing fashion, I remembered something from my past life: the amount of gaudy underwear I'd never seen before multiplying in my wife's dresser drawer.

Meanwhile, ignorant to my musings, Nias was floundering, attempting to force herself into various sexy poses. I started to feel bad for her as I watched.

"My lord…" she crooned.

It's just too pitiful. I let my shoulders slump, and tears welled up in Nias's eyes.

"Why do you look disappointed? You couldn't stop staring at my chest before!"

"True, but I'm not in the mood right now." My mood had turned rotten, in fact, from remembering my past life. At night, my wife wouldn't want to be intimate, yet she kept buying all that lingerie. It was the first thing that made me suspect she could be having an affair, but I'd decided to believe in her and avoided grilling her about it.

Apparently thinking she needed to redouble her efforts, Nias undid some of the buttons on her blouse and opened her legs enough that her panties were visible. She attempted to win me over with poses she was clearly not used to making, so embarrassed by her own efforts that she had flushed crimson.

"W-won't you *please* buy some battleships, my lord?" She affected a smile but was trembling slightly from all her strain.

The sight did nothing for me. Seeing a competent, cool beauty begging like this, something she'd normally never do, should have excited me, right? But all I felt for Nias at this moment was pity. She'd ended up eliciting a reaction from me after all, but what she'd stimulated was my compassion instead of my sex drive.

"Enough. It hurts to watch this, so I'll buy some already. It was two hundred, right?"

"Oh, I would appreciate it if you could buy three hundred!"

So now it's three hundred! She is way *too determined. And her seduction didn't even work.*

"Amagi, can we afford three hundred ships?" I asked, and Amagi performed the calculations immediately, supplying me with the answer.

"If we buy fewer ships than we originally considered, yes. From a long-term standpoint, I believe there will be no detriment to purchasing these vessels at this time."

I looked back at Nias to find her clasping her hands together, eyes aglimmer.

"Thank you so much! I'll have them delivered immediately."

"Wait. I'll buy them, but...do something about the exteriors, seriously. I don't care if it's just for show; put some sort of cover on the outside, even. You can think of something, can't you? I'll pay you to do something about the interiors too—they're just too cheap."

As we discussed the deal, Nias patted her chest in relief and pushed her glasses up, restoring their position. *You can try to look professional now, but I'm not gonna forget that sorry sight I just witnessed.*

"You can't understand the beauty of our functional designs?"

"Look, you need to understand how your potential customers feel, and why you're losing in trials."

Nias, who was sitting atop a table she'd leapt onto during her awkward show, slumped and hugged her knees to her chest.

"I know, and it really bothers me. I honestly tried talking to my bosses about all this, but they won't hear it."

You know I can still see your underwear, right? Maybe don't sit on top of a table.

Amagi never really showed much emotion, but there was almost some exasperation written on her face. "It appears her work is the only area she excels in," she remarked.

And she's so pretty too. A waste of beauty, that's what she is.

Leaving the business particulars to Amagi and Nias to discuss, I exited the reception room feeling exhausted.

Brian strolled the halls of the mansion.

"It's nice that we get so many visitors these days."

Before, no one wanted to visit the mansion due to the nobility's poor opinion of House Banfield. The fact that they were getting visitors now meant that people were starting to think well of Liam, and that thought elated Brian.

In these good spirits, he turned a corner and caught a woman's voice. "Hm?"

Is that our guest, Miss Nias? He knew it was rude, but he hid and listened discreetly to her conversation.

"Well, I managed to sell three hundred!"

She seemed to be addressing one of her coworkers at the Seventh Weapons Factory. From his vantage point, Brian could also see the floating screen that Nias was talking to.

"But that's with a condition to change the designs, though. The boss-men aren't gonna like that."

"W-well, what was I supposed to do? He wouldn't buy them otherwise! We just have to spruce 'em up a bit!"

Nias seemed unhappy with her coworker's response. "How hard do you think I had to work just to achieve that? Think about what I had to go through!"

"Honestly, I can't believe a straight arrow like you managed to pull off a seduction strategy, of all things. How far did you have to go, anyway?"

"Not as far as you're thinking, at least. But trust me, the count's head over heels for me. His eyes were all over me today—really."

"Really?"

"W-well, probably. I think." Nias's voice grew quieter and quieter as she lost confidence.

"Maybe you should just aim to become countess while you're at it."

"I'm not gonna go that far. Anyway, you should show me more respect! My wiles won us this deal, after all!"

"It's only three hundred ships, though, right? We've gotta sell a lot more than that."

"It's a start, isn't it? Can't you just say 'thank you'?"

From the conversation, Brian surmised that House Banfield would be purchasing three hundred battleships from the Seventh Weapons Factory. Although Brian had no choice but to obey his master's orders, there was one thing about the decision that he just couldn't accept: the fact that Nias had obviously seduced Liam into buying those ships.

Master Liam fell into a honey trap?
Brian was filled with anxiety for Liam's future.

7 Evil Merchant

"ECHIGOYA, you're quite wicked yourself!"

A lot of people probably knew this line. In my past life, the stereotypical "evil merchant" in media was usually named Echigoya. *Wonder how the real Echigoya feels about that.*

Before I get up to any mischief as an evil lord, I'll need to introduce you to my Echigoya—or rather, my personal purveyor of goods. He was a plump man with a mustache, the spitting image of an evil merchant, named Thomas Henfrey.

After I had shaped my crumbling domain into a more developed planet, Thomas came here to do business with me. By "business," I meant interplanetary trade. I wasn't sure I needed my own *personal* merchant in a society where there was spaceflight, but Thomas was one of those businessmen who were able to travel between planets.

He and his fellows did business not just within the Empire, but with worlds in other intergalactic networks. Basically, they could bring rare resources or goods from planets that were incredibly distant. Thus, these merchants were hugely different from the ones who operated solely within my domain. It was important for the continued development of my territory that I deal with their kind.

As I sat across from Thomas in my reception room, a low table between us, I asked, "Did you bring those yellow sweets with you?"

Thomas wiped sweat from his brow and handed me a case filled with bars of gold—the "yellow sweets." In other words, a bribe. This was indispensable for an exchange between an evil lord and an evil merchant. I'd seen it countless times in historical dramas in the past, so I was sure of it. Thomas wore a troubled look on his face, so I was sure it had taken some effort to scrape up this much.

"Of course. Please enjoy, my lord."

I accepted the case, and its weight in my hands caused me to grin. I felt my lips curling into a smile from the heavy weight of it. Mimicking the dialogue I'd seen between nefarious stock characters countless times over, I declared, "Echigoya, you're quite wicked yourself!"

"As I keep telling you, my lord, we are the Henfrey Company."

Thomas replied in the same way he always did, so I decided to stop messing around.

"Just joking."

"R-right. Naturally."

Our scripted exchange came to an end.

"So," I said, "I assume you didn't just come to say hi." Since he'd brought me a bribe, I was certain he needed a major favor.

"Well, I have to pass through a bit of an unsafe sector for a deal, so I was hoping I could borrow one of your fleets for protection. One hundred ships would do it, I think."

So he wants my military to protect him. I'm sure that's just an excuse, though, and he actually wants to use my muscle for some evil scheme. Well, as long as I'll profit, I don't mind lending my services.

"Are you going somewhere that dangerous?"

"It's not the place I'm *going* to that's dangerous. To get there, I have to pass through an area with numerous pirate bases. There are merchants who have been attacked two or three times in a single day in that region."

Space pirates were a troublesome bunch, and the type of trouble they caused varied wildly. There were small-time people who'd whip out weapons from generations past, and then there were the real dangerous types, like deserters from the military. Guys like that also worked as mercenaries and had real combat experience. Pirate fleets that had plenty of personnel and a good amount of decent equipment that posed an extreme threat.

I shot a glance at Amagi, who was waiting behind me, and she picked up on what I wanted to ask. "I will ready one hundred ships at once."

Looking back at Thomas, I nodded. "Very well. I'll help you out, but you know what I want in return, hm?"

Thomas gave a relieved sigh, but he still seemed nervous. "O-of course I do, but...er, I'll bring some more yellow sweets the next time I visit."

"Those are important, yes, but what's *most* important is that I profit. You'll make sure I do, won't you?" *If I'm not going to make anything from this, there's no point in lending him my military strength.*

"O-of course, my lord!"

"Okay, then! Amagi, make the arrangements."

"Certainly."

As my personal purveyor, you'll make sure I profit, won't you, Echigoya—I mean, Henfrey Company? I'm sure you'll be using me, so I'll just use you as well.

After his meeting with Liam, Thomas headed for the planet's orbital spaceport, where his large transport vessel was docked. House Banfield's spaceport was doughnut-shaped, with intricate webs of passageways leading to spaceship docks. As House Banfield increased in scale, its spaceport was also under constant renovation.

Thomas took a shuttle into space from the planet's surface and soon arrived at the spaceport. He had a bag in hand and an entourage of subordinates and guards. The spaceport was all moving walkways, so you could get to your destination just by standing still. Annoyingly, some vessels had to dock farther away from the spaceport's main body, but with Thomas's connections to House Banfield, he was allowed a convenient spot.

The ceilings of the passages to the docked ships were dome-shaped and allowed one to see the view beyond. Everyone peered up at Liam's planet, which loomed directly above them.

Evidently bored by the journey, one of Thomas's subordinates piped up, "House Banfield's domain sure has advanced, huh? I'm impressed that this count could restore so much of it at his young age."

Thomas had visited House Banfield's territory for business a number of times in the past. The planet had indeed seen rapid growth over the last few decades, enough that he hardly recognized it as the same place. Surmising that the reason for the planet's quick growth was its new lord, Liam, Thomas had decided to pursue a position as House Banfield's personal merchant. Before Liam, House Banfield had lacked financial credit. In fact, it was in the red, and no merchants would deal with it. It might've seemed high-risk for Thomas to attach himself to Liam, but by now he felt he was achieving some hefty returns.

"He's different from other nobles. There's something strange about him, but...he's a wise ruler."

No one around him objected to that judgment. Considering Liam demanded bribes at every meeting, how could he have been deemed wise? The Empire's values might have had something to do with it.

Still, the subordinate looked puzzled. "Why does he always demand gold, though? It's not a resource his territory is particularly lacking, is it? Sure, it's a precious metal, but doesn't he require anything else?"

Thomas didn't actually know the answer to that himself, so he wasn't sure how to respond. "I've often wondered that too—why gold? I even feel a bit bad. Not that I'm complaining. Once I presented him with some mithril and magical gems, but he wasn't satisfied. He's always excited to receive gold, though."

This universe was a fantasy world of swords and magic, and as such, there were plenty of more precious metals: mithril, adamantite, orichalcum, and so on. There were also magical gemstones and various treasures more valuable than gold. And yet, gold was all Liam desired. To Thomas, it was as if Liam were delighted at receiving a measly souvenir every time he visited. Its worth just didn't match up with the benefits Thomas was seeing from their relationship.

His subordinates were just as confused as he. "What an odd person."

They would never understand why Liam demanded gold, and how could they? It was only because in his previous life, on Earth, gold had possessed great value. However, that value came from the fact that there was a limited amount of it. In this world, gold had some value as a precious metal, but not nearly as much as something like mithril, a silver metal imbued with holy power. Usually, one would be happy to receive something like mithril, and since it was rarer than gold, it was treated as more valuable.

"He's a very humble person, I suppose."

Compared to the benefits Thomas saw as the personal merchant of House Banfield, the bribes Liam demanded were mere pocket change—a drop in the bucket. Thomas actually felt guilty about it.

Arriving at the end of the connecting passage, Thomas boarded his ship. "This station's really got all the conveniences now, hasn't it?"

As his ship left the spaceport, Thomas gazed back at it. The upgraded facilities boasted so much in the way of accommodations that things were starting to get a bit crowded. There were plans to build a second spaceport, and House Banfield would no doubt continue to thrive. Thomas was ever impressed at the amount Liam poured into his domain.

"I've heard he invests almost all of the taxes he collects. He makes it seem so easy, and to do it all at his age... He's something special, all right. Just imagine the state this place would be in if House Banfield didn't have all that debt."

He glanced at his subordinates. "This deal will be more dangerous than our usual ventures, but it will be very important for House Banfield. We'll make a nice profit here, and it's our turn to give back to our employer."

It would in fact be greatly beneficial to House Banfield if the Henfrey Company succeeded in their current venture. The firm had no reason to brave such danger for its own sake, but Thomas sincerely desired to give back to Liam after how kindly the count had treated him.

He was not an evil merchant.

Brian had come to Liam's office. "Another bribe, Master Liam?"

"I'm within my rights, am I not?"

"It's an enviable position to be in, sure, but..."

After finishing with his work, Liam had been admiring the gold he'd received from Thomas, the bars all lined up on his desk. Brian wished he could speak up more about Liam accepting these bribes so openly. *He seems so happy to receive it. Is he being humble?*

Liam was discussing how to make use of the gold with Amagi.

"Gold really is the ultimate treasure. What do you think, Amagi?"

Beside him, Amagi was preparing him some tea. "I believe it suffices. However, may I ask why you desire gold, Master?"

"Hmm?"

Brian found himself nodding. *Yes, there's the question! Why gold specifically? I really am curious.*

Liam gazed at a gold bar in his hand, his expression appearing somewhat lonesome. "I guess it's a symbol of the *nouveau riche*. And gold has real value too, value that won't change. You don't think that's wonderful?"

Amagi and Brian exchanged glances, and this time, Brian spoke up. "Er, Master Liam?"

"What is it?"

"You're aware that things like mithril have much more value than gold, yes?"

"Huh? Of course I am."

"Th-then, why not request mithril?"

Liam set down the bar of gold and gave a heavy sigh.

His lord's sheer disappointment startled Brian. "Have I made some mistake?"

"Nothing *but* mistakes. Where's the fun in showing off rare metals like mithril, orichalcum, and adamantite?"

Brian, personally, would have been elated to receive them. "Well, women like to receive mithril rings, do they not?"

"That's not what I'm asking! Mithril and orichalcum, for instance, have value because you can use them to make things, right? They're not just for show." According to Liam, other metals had no use as decorations.

Amagi agreed with him. Those metals had value because they were useful. "A reasonable judgment."

Brian also saw his reasoning and decided not to say anything further in response. Instead, he spoke about gold. "That is true. However, gold was a symbol of success in ancient times due to its scarcity, and it took on all sorts of other meanings as well. Don't you think it's rather superstitious to treasure it?"

Liam wasn't very interested in superstition. With a thoughtful hum, he said, "Well, whatever the case, we're going to make these into gold coins. Brian, take them to be minted."

"Master Liam, need I remind you that I am your *butler?* But very well, I'll get to it."

Things never really go according to plan. When I was a child in my past life, everyone had the idea that in the future we'd have flying cars, but when you grew up, you realized that even if flying cars existed, they wouldn't be commonplace. Even in an intergalactic empire, the view from a high-rise building—the penthouse of a classy hotel, for instance—wasn't that different from the sort of views I saw in my past life. In fact, I'd go so far as to say the metropolises of my past life were more developed than this. There were high-rises here, but they weren't crammed together. It sounded nice to say my planet was "teeming with nature," but in all honesty, there was just a lot of undeveloped land.

"We're still pretty much the sticks," I grumbled.

Amagi, who was at my side, replied, "Your domain has developed by leaps and bounds since you took over the peerage, Master. So much progress has been made that the planet is nearly unrecognizable from how it was when you became lord."

It was just like Amagi to think that way, but humans were all about appearances, and to me, this planet was still the boondocks.

"That's just what the numbers say, right? It doesn't mean anything if it doesn't feel that way to me. It's not the sight I want to see. The fashions are all off too—that's why I never want to take any women home with me."

Sometimes, I'd walk through my domain and think about picking up some girls, but their styles just weren't right for me. Lately, the women in my territory had started using their extra money to dress up and go shopping, but it still wasn't what I envisioned.

It's like being in the modern era and seeing fashion from a generation ago. That's not gonna get anyone excited! I like pure ladies, so how am I supposed to be interested if everyone's dressed like fashionistas? Basically, no one's my type, so

I'm never in the mood! At this rate, I won't be able to use my authority to drag women back to my mansion with me.

"We need to develop more. Especially in fashion."

"Is there really such a dire need?"

Cultures differed too much between planets in this world. Planets in the Empire shared a number of similarities, but too many things set them apart. I found some planets ideal, but I had to shake my head at many of their fashion choices. I mean, even on Earth, there were a ton of different cultures between countries. Expand the scope to multiple planets, and there was going to be even more variance.

"I know—I'll recruit some fashion designers or something like that. We've gotta invest in, uhh, cosmetology too! If we don't, my appetite will never get going!"

It wasn't just the everyday wear on this planet I had a problem with. When people went to the beach, they wore full-body swimsuits. My fantasy certainly didn't involve young people frolicking on the beach with only their faces exposed. *Are you kidding me?! Where's the fun in that?! Why don't you show some skin, people?! Unacceptable!*

"I want models here too. If people are shown beauty, it's sure to influence them. Let's have some famous people come visit!"

While I was throwing these new ideas out there, Amagi looked troubled. Maid robots didn't have a wide range of facial expressions, but I could decipher the slight changes in hers by now. We'd been together for over forty years at this point, after all.

She said, "Our debt continues to pose problems for us. We may be collecting more taxes now, but that means we are also making larger payments. I cannot approve of any significant investments at present."

I still couldn't do what I really wanted because of House Banfield's crushing debt. As I gazed out the window, a ship flew by, heading for space from the surface. This was probably the only futuristic sight you could see in my domain. True, it was more developed here than when I was five, but it was a dismal sight to me. This was just too far from my ideal world.

"Reality sure is boring."

Amagi showed me some holographic images. She had searched up a number of fashion designers and models we could afford to hire.

"If you must bring designers and models here, we may be able to hire these individuals."

I took a look at the images, and this time they were super futuristic. Rather, they were too unique for me to consider. *Why would you wear a spinning hula hoop around your waist? The hair is striking, sure, but with such a weird shape, doesn't it get in the way? This is the latest fashion? It's not, like, for some costume contest? What exactly is fashion, anyway?*

"This isn't what I was expecting."

Responding to my dissatisfaction, Amagi moved on to the next set of images. "How about these? They are all popular models in the Empire."

"What is this?"

I found the models' styles even more striking, but only because certain parts of their bodies were exaggerated. Their breasts, their butts—they varied from extremely large to extremely small in different combinations.

"On this planet, South, a woman is considered more attractive the larger her breasts are. For that reason, these women are South's top models."

The breasts of the models in question were immense. *Too big! They're so huge, I can't even find them attractive.*

"Those are way too big! How do they even go about their day when they're built like that?"

I like big boobs, but I don't want breasts so gigantic that they'd be a hindrance in a woman's daily life. No, I don't even know if you can call these breasts anymore.

Amagi dispassionately explained, "To the men in South, these women are irresistible. In South, a woman's appeal lies entirely in her bust."

"Guess that's why they don't put focus on anything else."

Next, Amagi showed me an image of men surrounding these models. There were noticeably larger crowds around the women with oversized chests. I simply couldn't understand the enthusiasm, the obsession with breasts and nothing else.

"Denizens of this next planet value the nape of the neck over—"

"That's enough!"

I didn't understand the scale of an intergalactic society well enough.

The universe truly is vast.

House Banfield's space army was undergoing training. Its commander was the brigadier general who had come from the Imperial Army. In House Banfield's military, he'd been assigned the rank of lieutenant general, which was two ranks higher. His vessel was a cutting-edge battleship, the likes of which he never would've had in the Imperial Army. There were some flaws in its interior design, but its specs were truly magnificent.

"Lord Banfield is quite generous," the general remarked.

The general's adjutant, a former major treated as a colonel by House Banfield, had a mouth on him, but he was a capable subordinate. He'd been booted out here to House Banfield's realm because his previous superior hadn't liked his sarcastic comments.

"Couldn't agree more," he said. "We're treated a hell of a lot better here than we were in the army. I'm almost grateful to the top brass for demoting us. Not that you'd ever catch me thanking those guys."

By Imperial standards, House Banfield was the boonies, but it was a comfortable enough place to live. It was no bustling metropolis, but the planet was more developed than other backwater territories they'd been to. Not only were the soldiers treated well, but the army functioned like a well-oiled machine.

"Mind your mouth, would you, Colonel? In any case, the fleet's quality, numbers, and capabilities are all fine, wouldn't you say?"

Each ship was staffed by just the right amount of personnel, and they all got regular training and time off. Altogether, they functioned perfectly as a fleet.

"Feels a lot more fulfilling than languishing out on the frontier. Everyone always looks cheerful. I suppose the only problem is that we have to sortie a bit more than I'd like."

They'd been battling space pirates more frequently as of late. As the planet developed more and more, it became a bigger target for nearby pirates, and getting rid of them was one of the military's jobs.

"We're paid more than enough for the work."

"True enough! Lord Banfield's pretty much the ideal ruler, especially compared to these nobles who say to just ignore pirates."

"Quite. He's already being called a wise ruler at his age, and I must say I agree."

Some Empire nobles got involved with pirates and would tell their military to ignore them. It was frustrating for the soldiers, but Liam would never have done such a thing, hence his military's esteem for him.

"He's not even an adult yet, right? I thought all nobles were rotten, but when I see him, I kinda have to wonder what was wrong with our old superiors."

"Lord Banfield is a true noble. We're lucky to be able to serve under him."

Before, the soldiers had felt they'd been abandoned by the military, but they'd actually been given a superior who would put their full talents to use. They were all highly motivated in their new stations.

For the first time in a while, a door between worlds opened, and the Guide slipped through. As soon as he saw Liam's current situation, however, the Guide was appalled.

"He hasn't done anything!"

He'd thought Liam was planning on engaging in debauchery, but he hadn't touched liquor or women. Abstaining from liquor was fine considering he wasn't yet of age, but the reason he wasn't indulging in the company of women was his mistrust of them, and because he couldn't find anyone he was attracted to on his planet.

In no time at all, Liam had worked his way to becoming a proper ruler. The state of his domain had improved with each of the Guide's visits.

"I'm immensely disappointed. I was so looking forward to this, and now I feel betrayed. Why is he being treated like a wise leader when he's supposed to be aiming for evil lord?"

The Guide also couldn't accept the small luxuries Liam enjoyed because of his past-life sensibilities. The kid was actually pretty satisfied with his life now, so he had plenty of room in his heart—room that was currently devoted to gratitude for the Guide.

To make things even more frustrating, Liam's populace adored him too. The appreciation amplified the pleasant feelings in his heart—the exact opposite of what the Guide had hoped to savor. These emotions sickened him, and he was plagued by heartburn, headaches, nausea, and dizziness. He could endure the physical repercussions, but he couldn't shed his agitation.

In the end, the Guide planned to throw Liam down into hell eventually one way or another, so he didn't mind it all *too* much. However, with the way things were, the future the Guide desired would never arrive no matter what happened. If he left things alone, Liam was sure to be a sensible lord until his last breath.

"What a letdown. At this rate, nothing rewarding is going to happen."

He'd wanted to see the people stewing in dissatisfaction for their evil lord, the military plotting a rebellion, the women Liam had forced to his side wishing to kill him. Instead, the people practically revered their humble lord, the military had devoted their lives to him, and Liam didn't even have any women at his side—meaning there was nothing to stir up his bitter memories of his past life.

Is he really trying to be evil? the Guide wondered, doubtful.

"Well, let's at least topple this domain he's built up before it's all over. I see there are some space pirates nearby who should do the trick."

Black smoke spilled out from the Guide's form and dissolved into the air around him. He looked down at Liam with cold eyes, and said with a voice just as frigid, "I hope you can at least entertain me at the end. I'm going to stay right here and enjoy the rest of the show."

A storm of missiles rained down upon a planet far from House Banfield's domain, creating massive explosions on the surface and charring the earth to ash. From the bridge of a nearby space vessel, a pirate watched the devastation of the beautiful planet.

This man, who commanded a fleet of more than thirty thousand pirate ships, was named Goaz. He'd named the fleet after himself, calling it the Goaz Pirate Gang, and they had a hefty bounty on their heads. His black beard, bulging muscles, and scarred, shaved head made him look rugged. He laughed heartily, swigging liquor from a bottle clutched in his fist as he watched the carnage below.

"I can never get enough of this part!"

As Goaz chortled away, one of his lackeys couldn't help commenting, "Do we really have to go this far, Captain?"

Goaz clamped a huge hand on the man's head. Some of the surrounding pirates averted their eyes, while others looked on with disgust, thinking, *What an idiot.*

"And who told you to share your opinion, eh? Don't get in the way of my fun!"

"C-Captain, wai—!"

With just the one hand, he crushed the man's skull. Another lackey waiting nearby carefully wiped Goaz's hand clean. As his men carried the body out and cleaned up the area, Goaz resumed watching the planetary destruction from a monitor on the bridge.

He placed that same hand on a golden box he seemed to treasure. The box, which had a kind of crest on it, was always at his side. He kept it so close, in fact, that he carried it around in a special holster. He stroked the box gently now as though it were precious.

"Another easy job." That was his comment after destroying an entire planet and all the people who dwelt on it. To anyone, that line would have made the full extent of the man's villainy amply clear. Goaz also had a personal bounty on him, which was an incredible sum. If someone could take out Goaz and the Goaz Pirate Gang, they could live lavishly for the rest of their days and still have money to spare. That was how dangerous this man was.

Goaz's right-hand man spoke, trying not to upset him. "It was another big haul today, eh? By the way, what do you intend to do with that girl you took a liking to? You've got a new one now, so do you think it's time to get rid of her?"

Goaz grinned, showing his yellowed teeth. "Guess so. It's probably time to focus on the new toy. I did have a lot of fun with that one, though."

His adjutant had the same vulgar grin. "I'm surprised she managed to maintain her sense of self after being your toy, Boss. Anyway, what do you wanna do next? Take a nice vacation somewhere?"

Just as Goaz was about to agree, he saw some sort of black smoke. He rubbed his eyes, but it was gone, so he figured it had just been his imagination. Then he had a great idea. "No... Wait."

"Boss?"

"I've heard rumors lately of a brat around here who's gettin' a big head. What was his name—Banfield? They're callin' him a 'wise ruler.' Say he's workin' real hard out on this planet in the sticks."

His right-hand man also recalled those rumors and anticipated what Goaz wanted to say. "Yeah, I've been hearing a lot about him lately. So our next prey'll be Banfield, then?"

Goaz had nothing to fear from nobility—not with his special treasure, after all.

"There's nothin' better than tearing down something somebody spent a long time building, is there? Plus, this job ended too fast... I'm bored already."

His adjutant nodded. "Well, we'll set a course for House Banfield, then."

Goaz licked his lips. "Time to teach that arrogant little brat a lesson."

8 Space Pirates

MY FIFTIETH BIRTHDAY was approaching—the age at which people were considered adults in this world. Though I still looked like a kid, I was at the threshold of an important milestone. *I'm about to become an adult, but it took half a century to get here.*

At this age, I finally asked myself, "I was reincarnated into a science fiction world, so why the hell am I spending all my time cooped up in this mansion?"

"You are able to get an appropriate amount of exercise inside the mansion, and here you remain safe," Amagi replied matter-of-factly. She had ignored the whole "reincarnation" part, which I found impressive. "It would be more of a problem for you to leave."

Is she mad about that time I wanted to go out and pick up some girls? I didn't even go through with it, though. Seriously, what am I gonna do? If I want to become an

evil lord, I should be gulping down booze while beautiful women wait on me hand and foot. What else?

It feels wrong to drink it in this body, and it doesn't taste good anyway. I'm still developing, so I don't want to ruin that. Also, Amagi makes it hard for me to look at other women. If the ideal woman is always at your side, you end up comparing other people to her. Plus, it's not like there's any issue with not *having women around. Maybe there's no reason to go to all that effort?*

"No. I'm going to become an evil lord. I can't just give up here."

"Is that so? I have to say, I do not know how to react to that statement. What sort of things do you intend to do?"

"Uh, raise taxes and exploit my people?" *Evil lords are all about high taxes, right? That should be foremost, I think.*

"Our revenue would increase temporarily, but you would lose money in the long run, so I cannot recommend it. We can raise taxes judiciously, if necessary, but if our administration of the planet backslides, it will impact our debt repayment plans."

At times, it's better to lower taxes and get people buying more to increase revenue. There's nothing to be gained from forcing people to pay more taxes. No, wait... We're not just talking about economics here! I want to trample people underfoot! I don't want anything taken from me—I want to do the taking!

"I don't want to hear your reasonable opinions. I want to take stuff for myself, with authority and violence!"

That's right. I am the one who takes, and my people are there to be taken from. Forget about tax revenue!

"First off, I'll go find some beautiful women and bring them to the mansion. I'll stop nitpicking about fashion for now and just dress them up how I like once they're here."

Amagi cocked her head to one side. *What? What's the problem? Is she mad? W-well, I'm not giving up on this.*

"Got a problem, Amagi? I'm doing it anyway! Find some beautiful women in my domain!"

Her response caught me off guard. "Master, aside from those in technical positions, appearance was factored into selecting the people who work in the mansion. They were handpicked from across your domain."

"Huh?"

"The mansion is already full of beautiful women. They have long since been found."

When that sank in, I pictured the people who worked here. It was true: there were handsome men and beautiful women all around me. Now that I thought about it, all the maids who saw to my needs were gorgeous.

Seeing the consternation on my face, Amagi asked, "Shall I select someone to...attend to you?"

"No, I'm not really in the mood. Wait, huh? I can do that?"

I couldn't hide my surprise. *Is that really allowed? What, I could have just done whatever I wanted this whole time? I mean, I totally wanted to! I might have already if Amagi hadn't been around.*

"It is something taken into account when hiring staff. If you would prefer a man, I can arrange for that as well."

"Not for me, thanks."

Do you think I'm interested in men? Anyway, it's no fun having my way with women if I'm entitled to it. The fun is in compelling them!

"Then I'll bring some entertainers here from around my domain! What I really want is to make someone submit to me."

"Master, your domain does not yet have a robust entertainment industry. Also, I doubt that a summons from you would make many people upset. You are the best possible patron on this planet. Would you like to bring people in from outside your domain? To be frank, I think many of them would also come happily."

Outside? Like, from other territories?

"I want to enjoy being the king of my own kingdom—people from outside wouldn't be my subjects! It could be bad if they snuck off afterward and told others what I was doing."

I don't want to start any conflicts with other territories when I don't have enough power yet. I'll wait until I'm stronger to do that. You can't be an evil lord without cunning.

"Please do not worry, Master; you are the ruler of House Banfield. You already are the king of your own kingdom."

I mean, I know that, but that's not what I mean! Dammit... Is it really this hard to be an evil lord?

"None of my plans are going anywhere. What am I supposed to do? Why is my goal to go down the path of evil, debauchery, and female servants so impossible to achieve?"

Then, Amagi reminded me of the root of the problem: "I suppose it is difficult to live extravagantly with such a large debt."

No matter how much progress my domain makes, as long as I have this debt hanging over me, I can't do as I please. But if I slow down any more on repaying it, the collectors are gonna be pissed, and if they see I'm living it up while I owe them so much, they'll get serious and come after me.

Suddenly I'm remembering the fear I felt in my past life.

"Dammit... Isn't there some easy way for me to repay it?"

"I am afraid there is little to be done about that. We should continue to pay it back diligently. If they see that we are making an effort, they will not press us to pay more than we can afford."

That was when I received an emergency transmission from Brian.

"Why not just report to my office?" I authorized the transmission and an image appeared in the air before me.

"Master Liam, it's terrible! P-p-p-pirates have declared war against House Banfield!"

That's awfully formal of them, considering they're pirates.

"Pirates, notifying us of war, Amagi. Isn't that decent of them?"

"It is just as decent of you to diligently repay your debts even though you aim to be an evil lord, Master."

"Well, those debts are crippling me, so I've taken care of 'em."

"A valid point. As for the matter of the pirates, if they are declaring war, they must be quite unintelligent...or perhaps the exact opposite."

Completely confident, in other words.

In my domain loomed a government administration building. Unlike my mansion, it was a high-rise, towering over its surrounding buildings ostentatiously to express my prestige.

The officials who governed my domain worked there, and I visited every so often. Being the highest man on the totem pole, I usually just had them come to my mansion if they needed me for something. Since most of our correspondence was remote, it had been a long time since I'd physically come to the government building.

They really didn't have to build this thing so huge.

All the important people in my domain were gathered there in a meeting room, discussing the pirates' declaration of war and their demands. These officials in suits nervously went over the details.

"The pirates are demanding that we hand over all of our wealth, along with some attractive men and women."

I studied the list of precious metals they wanted and determined we couldn't produce what they were asking for. And they only wanted good-looking people for their hostages? That pissed me off. Why the hell should I have to hand over my property to them?

"Lord Banfield, should we try to negotiate with the pirates so we can take care of this peacefully?"

The military brass participating in the meeting didn't like the weak-willed attitude of the government officials. They didn't want to concede defeat to the pirates.

"We're up against Goaz! He's got a huge bounty on his head!"

Apparently, this pirate threatening us was a big-time villain. If we managed to take down his whole fleet, we could obtain an unimaginable sum of money.

I wonder what the guy did to get such a huge bounty placed on him.

The blood of the military men began to boil as the official's eyes turned ice-cold.

"Can you win? If we scrounge together House Banfield's entire fighting force, it's eight thousand ships. Goaz commands a fleet of thirty thousand!"

"Numbers aren't everything—our forces are experienced and well equipped! Besides, do you really think they're just going to let us be if we give up and surrender?"

"Are you sure you're not just planning to escape by yourselves? All you have to do is get in your ships and leave."

"How dare you!"

As their argument grew heated, I contemplated Goaz's bounty. It wasn't actually that much for a count like me. A decent amount of money, sure, but it wasn't going to bury me in riches. *What a shame.*

I sighed. "If the bounty were a little higher, I'd be a little more motivated."

Nobody paid attention to my muttering, the argument still raging.

Suddenly, the clamor around me abruptly cut out. I looked up and was confronted with a strange sight. All the people who had just been arguing so fiercely were now frozen in place, not moving an inch. It was as though time had come to a halt.

For a second, I thought maybe it was just some sort of prank, but they wouldn't have been stupid enough to pull that with me. I'd kill them if they did. *I'll never let anyone make a fool of me.* While I was thinking that, I heard an old, familiar voice.

"Well, hello."

"It's you!"

"Allow me to take a moment of your time. *Stopping* time is pretty tiring, incidentally. Anyway, it's been a while, hasn't it, Liam?"

Nostalgia welled up in me when I saw the Guide, unchanged from how he'd looked before I was reincarnated. However, there was a more pressing matter at hand than the exchange of pleasantries.

"Long time no see. By the way, what's going on here? I'm being attacked by pirates."

Weren't you supposed to be making me happy? I left that part implied.

The corners of the Guide's mouth tugged up in a smile. "You've misunderstood my intentions. This is a present for you, Liam."

"A present?"

"Yes. You're soon reaching adulthood in this world, correct? I wanted to grant you some prestige as a noble before then. Plus, you're saddled with a bit of a debt here, isn't that true?"

That *was* true, but it pissed me off, so I gave him a bit of a grouchy answer. I wanted him to understand that I'd had a hard time because of him.

"Yup. And thanks to that, I haven't been able to do what I want here. It would've been nice if you'd placed me in a wealthier family. So why'd you pick this place?"

The Guide looked a bit remorseful. "Please allow me to apologize for that. In order to correct this situation, I've invited some pirates with a sizable fortune to your territory. If you defeat them, all their treasure will be yours."

"Treasure, you say?"

The Guide stepped closer, rubbing his hands together. "Yes, that's right. If you take them down, you'll obtain fame *and* ample fortune. The leader of these pirates holds an incredible treasure, and I sent him your way so you could have it."

"Oh yeah? Well, I'm looking forward to that, then."

I smiled at him, and the Guide grinned back, though I found it unsettling.

"I'm glad you understand. Those pirates are no match for you as you are now, Liam. So, now that I've followed up with you, I'll just be going."

Raising the brim of his top hat, the Guide bowed deeply, and a door appeared behind him. As usual, I couldn't see any part of his face other than his mouth.

"Thanks for coming all this way."

For a second, it looked like the smile had disappeared from his face, but it quickly returned.

"All part of the job."

The Guide passed through the door and closed it after him, then it vanished.

A moment later, the loud argument around me blasted back into motion. Now that time had resumed, it seemed ridiculous to me that these guys were so afraid of these pirates, who I now knew were a nice little present for me.

When I stood up from my seat, all the eyes in the meeting room turned to me.

"I think this is a great opportunity for me to experience my first battle. Get everything ready—I'm going to crush Goaz."

At my pronouncement, the officials *and* the soldiers began to panic. They had just been at odds a moment ago, but now they seemed to share some sort of understanding. They probably hadn't been expecting that I'd want to engage the pirates myself.

"Lord Banfield, that's reckless. These are renowned pirates. There are even former knights in their ranks, but House Banfield doesn't have a knight to its name. The pirates' forces easily surpass ours."

We boasted no families who had served House Banfield for generations, nor new retainers recruited from elsewhere. There were likely no knights who felt there was any benefit in serving House Banfield. But, I told myself, this wasn't a problem. If the Guide had arranged it, there was no way I could lose.

"Be that as it may, I said I'm doing it. All you have to worry about is getting everything ready for me. I've given you an order. Now, hold your objections and follow my command."

The military men still seemed a little displeased, but the officials had all gone quiet, remembering the purge I'd carried out several years ago.

That's right, just shut up and do what I say. If you listen to me, I'll use you well. And if you don't—you'll die.

"Gather up all the fighting power you can. I'll be piloting the Avid."

One of the soldiers—a commander from the force pulled from the Imperial Army—still had an objection.

"It's too dangerous for you to fight, lord. We should wait for reinforcements from the Imperial Army. Please wait planetside—"

"Wait for reinforcements? Will they make it in time?"

We had in fact requested aid from the Empire, but it would take time for them to amass a force and send it out here to the sticks. I couldn't imagine they'd arrive before the pirates attacked.

"I imagine it will be close, but if we have any hope of winning, our only option is to wait for reinforcements."

I'm not gonna just sit here and wait for help. Plus, if the Empire shows up, my share of the treasure will decrease.

"We can't wait for aid that may not even make it in time. If we don't engage the pirates, they'll just destroy us. I would rather go on the offensive. Just carry out my orders, all of you—we're doing some pirate hunting. I was looking for an opportunity to take part in my first battle anyway, so this works out perfectly."

It's fun playing a game when you know you'll win. No, this isn't even a game—it's a one-sided hunt. These pirates have come bearing prestige and a lavish treasure that's mine for the taking. Let's go greet them.

"Begin the offensive."

In the mansion, Brian was having a hard time remaining calm.

"The Avid has arrived at the spaceport," Amagi reported to him. "It will be loaded onto the same ship Master is boarding."

Brian doubled over, head between his hands, bemoaning the misfortune that had come to House Banfield. The family had finally found a good ruler in Liam, but with his reign just beginning to bloom, a notorious pirate gang had flown in to attack their planet.

"What ill fortune—the planet was finally regaining its former vitality. Why have these terrible space pirates chosen now of all times to attack?"

Amagi showed no outward signs of anxiety, but she seemed concerned for Liam at the very least.

"We have not lost yet. Master's decision was the right one. Based on records of this pirate gang's previous conquests, surrender would be meaningless. Additionally, we received a message that the Empire will be dispatching the regular army."

Brian shook his head. Even hearing that the regular army was coming didn't comfort him.

"They won't make it. By the time they put a force together and send it out here, it will all be over."

When dangerous pirates entered Empire territory, provincial lords called on the Empire for help, but House Banfield was far into the outskirts. In his mind, he could imagine the flow of events: the pirates would wreak havoc on their planet, and only after they left would the Imperial Army arrive.

"House Banfield was finally...*finally* getting back on its feet," he lamented. "If Lord Liam had just been born one hundred years earlier, he would have been able to repel these invaders."

The arrival of the pirates bitterly vexed Brian, who had been looking forward to Liam's future achievements. If only Liam had had more time to bolster his forces, his victory against the pirates would've been assured.

At House Banfield's spaceport, the Guide watched as Liam's fleet assembled. He stood on the main structure's outer wall, smiling as he looked down at the men hurriedly preparing for battle.

"I'm so glad you liked my present. As for me, I'll be just thrilled if the pirates capture you and have their way with you."

The Guide hadn't informed Liam that the Goaz Pirate Gang possessed far greater fighting strength than the average space pirate fleet, or that there was a secret to the treasure he had mentioned. That small box was the source of Goaz's fortune—the reason for his strength. Goaz had amassed an imposing force due to this treasure, and while their training might not have matched that of a proper military, they were far better equipped than a typical pirate gang. In fact, their equipment rivaled that of the Empire's regular army. The Guide had informed Liam of exactly none of this.

"It's your fault for believing in me. You didn't learn a single thing in your past life, did you? Turns out you're nothing but a fool after all, destined to be a toy for others to mess with."

With their superior numbers, the pirates had an overwhelming advantage in this fight. Liam's chance of besting them was infinitesimally small. Scowling, the Guide recalled his conversation with Liam.

"I can't believe he thanked me. I look forward to seeing his face later. Soon, his gratitude will turn to resentment and his smile will warp with hatred. That's sure to satisfy me, at last."

He was eagerly awaiting Liam's fall from grace.

Behind him, a small light that had been keeping watch over him left his side and headed for the Avid, which had been stowed aboard the battleship. This small light entered the Avid, making sure the Guide didn't notice.

Unaware of this, the Guide spread his arms. "Oh, I do so look forward to watching this play out. Now, Liam, it's finally time for you to learn the truth! Please entertain me, won't you?"

Why had he reincarnated Liam into this life? Why had Liam's previous life been so miserable? The Guide could hardly wait to inform Liam of the answers to these questions.

9 First Battle

W E'D BEEN ABLE to scrape up some five thousand ships. Although our full military force consisted of eight thousand ships, between vessels in maintenance and those that simply couldn't be readied in time, that was what we had to work with. If we'd waited a little longer, we might have been able to boost that number to six or seven thousand, but I didn't think we should delay any further.

On the bridge of my space battleship, I sat haughtily in my specially outfitted chair. The bridge was large, with over a hundred people scurrying around on it. Mine was a high-performance vessel, capable of serving as the command center for all five thousand of my ships. With the commanders and staff officers on board, it boasted more personnel than the average ship.

From my chair, I ordered the busy soldiers to pick up the pace. "Are we ready to launch yet?"

The soldiers were all on edge, but they couldn't talk back to a noble. This was just how things were in the Empire; the class divisions were absolute, and no one could disobey me. Frankly, it felt great. The lowly grunts worked like maniacs while I was sitting pretty at the top, watching them.

This is what it means to be nobility. Course, I'd be pissed if I were in their shoes. You're working hard and your boss is taking it easy? I'd wanna kill him.

"It won't be long now, my lord. More importantly, is this really the best course of action?"

The commanding officer once again questioned my orders, but I cut the conversation short with a curt "Enough."

This is a fixed game. Sure, I'm up against a huge pirate gang, but it's nothing but a bonus stage for me. My win's already been decided. I smirked. I couldn't wait to see my prize.

"These guys have some sort of treasure, right?"

The soldiers exchanged a glance at my sudden change in topic. "I-it seems so. From the way they run rampant, it would make sense that the Goaz Pirate Gang is in possession of some miraculous treasure."

I grinned. "I'm looking forward to taking it from them. I'm eager to make use of it."

They continued to gawk at me, baffled.

These guys are totally scared of the other side's numbers. Is it normal for my personal army to respond like this?

In the midst of all the nervous energy on the bridge, Liam alone was smiling. Sitting in the chair prepared for the count and no one else, he elegantly sipped his drink. He looked entirely calm, so no one was quite sure how to react.

"Pretty calm for his first battle," the mouthy colonel remarked to his commander, the lieutenant general.

The lieutenant general wasn't sure how to feel about Liam's attitude either. "It doesn't look like he's simply putting on a brave face."

His cohort was inclined to agree. "He has a reputation for being a capable administrator, but what about his military prowess? Personally, I'd prefer it if he didn't try to interfere too much."

"Agreed."

None of the soldiers knew what to think. It was rare for a lord to come to the front lines himself. Normally, nobles stayed safe in the rear or left their domains behind and fled. Yet Liam had said he would lead them into battle—and he wasn't even an adult yet.

"Maybe it's his brand of noble pride. I think it's commendable," the lieutenant general said, and the colonel nodded.

If they were to be honest, the soldiers would have preferred that Liam run and live to see another day, but it also gave them courage to watch him trying to do his duty.

"The troops are less jittery with our lord here. I hope he'll just keep sitting there and boosting morale."

From the soldiers' perspective, their ruler was fighting with them instead of abandoning ship. Some of them were deeply moved by the sight, thinking, *This is what a noble should be.*

Liam being on the battlefield also meant that his military personnel wouldn't be used as sacrificial pawns. Sacrificing soldiers so that the nobility could escape wasn't an unusual tactic in the Empire. As a result, House Banfield's private army had unexpectedly high morale. They were still able to hold on to their fighting spirit in the face of an enemy force six times their size.

Adjusting his hat, the lieutenant general steeled himself. "Now we have to make sure to follow his example ourselves."

"You said it."

Of the ships making up the Goaz Pirate Gang's fleet, Goaz commanded a particularly large vessel. It had belonged to a nation he'd destroyed, and he'd taken a liking to it. Of course, with all the modifications he'd made, it hardly resembled the original vessel anymore.

Having received a report on the bridge of this ship, Goaz pressed his hand to his brow and laughed. "He's comin' out himself? The little kid's gonna fight with the grown-ups?"

The other pirates made sure to join in his laughter to keep Goaz in a good mood. To date, the Goaz Pirate Gang had never known defeat. They had nothing to fear from a backwater count with a paltry number of soldiers and not a single knight. To them, Liam's actions seemed suicidal.

"Well, he's got guts, I'll give him that. Hey, tell everyone that they'll get twice the reward if they take him alive. I'm gonna make the kid my new toy."

Knowing exactly how Goaz liked to play with his toys, his adjutant grinned. "Great taste as always, Boss."

Goaz was in a great mood, enjoying Liam's response to his arrival. "It's nice to take down stuck-up brats like him. I think I'll torment his poor, defenseless people when I'm done with him."

For nearly a century, Goaz had toyed with countless people's lives. The reason he was able to accomplish all this was the small gold box he'd acquired—the alchemy box. This was the treasure that had transformed Goaz from some random thug into the captain of a tremendous pirate fleet.

The alchemy box was a fantastical item that could turn any old junk into gold. It had been created by an ancient craftsman, the secrets of its manufacturing lost to time. It was said that no one would ever be able to make anything like it again. It didn't just make gold either; the device could also transmute material into mithril or adamantite. With this item, any old stone lying by a roadside could become a precious metal. It was just that powerful.

"I think it's time we teach an ignorant little brat what a real war is all about."

In the pirates' minds, they had already won. It was only natural for them to feel this way, considering their forces were six times as large as their enemy's. They didn't even need a strategy. Ram into 'em head-on, and victory was certain.

Several days after departing my domain, we finally faced off against the pirates. I'd been listening to the lieutenant general, who was acting commander on my ship, give orders, but it was *so* boring that I struggled to stay awake. My captain's chair was really high quality. It didn't make my back hurt when I sat in it for hours, and it was so comfortable, it made me sleepy. In fact, I'd already fallen asleep in it several times over the last few days. If I let my guard down now, I would probably start snoozing again.

There was a reason for the boredom. Because both fleets knew the other's exact position, every move was too predictable. It had been days since we'd first encountered each other, but there hadn't yet been a battle. All either side had done during this time was reposition its ships into fresh battle formations. I didn't know anything about warfare, so I'd let my men do the work, but if I didn't say something soon, there might never *be* a battle.

I got the impression we were in for a hard fight because of our inferior numbers, but so far, it was just too quiet. *When's the fighting gonna start?*

I asked a nearby soldier just that. "So when will we go to battle?"

"It has already begun, my lord. In a fight of this scale, one cannot simply charge at the enemy. Being outnumbered, we're in a bit of a tight spot."

It hasn't even started yet and we're already in a tight spot? What's up with that?

"I don't see the enemy."

"In space, if you can see the enemy, you're at point-blank range."

"That does sound familiar." I felt like I'd learned it in the education capsule, but I'd never gotten a lesson from an actual soldier, so the memory eluded me.

These guys really don't suck up to me though, huh? I wouldn't mind if they did, but I guess I should value their frankness. They're doing good work for me, so I'll allow it. I guess they're just trying to gauge the right distance we should be from the enemy and the right time to close that distance. Really, this is a battle fought with instrumentation. Still, how long does it take to stare down the other guys?

"At that scale, they probably have some real military advisers," the commander muttered.

Neighboring soldiers were discussing the same. "I hear they've got a lot of former soldiers."

"With this difference in numbers, they'll be massive trouble if they're any better than incompetent."

I turned back to the soldier next to me. "Is this what all battles are like?"

"Not typically, no, but commanders always have to worry about the timing of their attacks."

Gradually, the two forces drew closer together and readjusted their formations. The enemy wasn't in visible range, but both sides were aware of the other. On a simplified 3D representation of the battlefield, I could see our enemies attempting to surround us.

"How long do we have to wait?" Just when I was thinking about ordering my fleet to charge already, I snapped alert at a shout from one of the bridge operators.

"Communications failure! Jamming is coming from… directly above the fleet! Enemies approaching from above! Five hundred of them!"

The commander calmly gave his orders. "Prepare to intercept, but don't let them distract you from the main force!"

My swiftly moving fleet turned, so that the ships' noses pointed upward at the attacking enemy.

Meanwhile, the commander grimaced. "So they made their move first."

I asked the soldier next to me to explain. "Shouldn't you avoid dividing your forces? Why would they attack us with only five hundred ships?"

"They're trying to break up our formation. No matter how quickly we intercept, they'll be able to throw us off somehow."

"They should just go all out from the start," I complained.

This soldier then noticed something about the charging enemies, and the color drained from his face.

"My lord, those aren't pirates... These are vessels that *surrendered* to the pirates. That's another territory's military—being used as sacrificial pawns."

These ships didn't look to be of the Empire, so they must have been from a different intergalactic nation.

"They capture an enemy force and send it at another enemy. Tell me, if they could cut off our communications, why didn't they do that first?"

"It would affect their own communications too. Think of it as something to be used only at a crucial moment."

If they couldn't communicate, they couldn't send orders. It would be a real pain for both sides.

When the charging fleet launched their attack, we intercepted and fired back at them. All sorts of beams streaked between us. There was some beauty in the flashes of light as they lit up the darkness of space.

Man, explosions in space... Gotta say, fantasy worlds are pretty amazing.

From his ship's bridge, Goaz applauded his enemy. "The brat can fight. Or he's got some talented people working for him."

They'd repelled five hundred of his allied ships, but

Goaz didn't care. The defeated troops were just fodder who'd surrendered to him, so it was no skin off his back to lose them. Plus, his advantage was so overwhelming that the loss of a mere five hundred ships would do nothing to affect the outcome of the battle.

His adjutant didn't look particularly bothered either. "Things are chaotic for them, Boss. Now's the time to attack."

House Banfield's fleet was already in disarray, and there was no way for them to regain their organization with communications down. While their detachment was doing battle, the pirates had advanced.

Goaz nodded at his adjutant's appraisal of the situation. His rousing voice reverberated through the bridge. "Time to charge, boys! While they're still confused, let's teach 'em how pirates do things!"

At Goaz's order, the full pirate fleet charged. They weren't in any kind of formation, but they didn't care. Considering how disorganized their enemy was, they could easily be defeated with just a head-on assault.

House Banfield's fleet retreated while staying in formation, the ships' noses still pointed at the enemy.

"They're running. We'll pursue, and... Hm?"

The attacking pirates had flown straight into a trap—a minefield. Fifty or so ships at the front of the charge got caught up in the blasts and were torn to pieces. The explosions even reached some ships behind them, creating significant damage.

"Sneaky."

They must have spread the mines as the two forces were facing off, or while they retreated. Whatever the case, in terms of their total fighting force, they hadn't lost that much.

Unbothered, the adjutant evaluated House Banfield's forces. "They're better than we thought."

Goaz was rather amused by their resistance. "It's better when they entertain us a bit. A few losses won't—"

Suddenly, their frontline ships were hit by an enemy barrage and began to explode.

"Huh?" Goaz raised an eyebrow and looked to his adjutant for an explanation.

The other man hurried to reply, looking anxious. "Their troops seem to be quite experienced, and their equipment isn't bad either."

Goaz clicked his tongue. They weren't able to confer with their other ships or intercept enemy transmissions with communications down for both sides, but from here, it appeared these guys were putting up a better fight than they'd expected. The tables had turned at the front lines.

"Pretty impressive, but what does it matter? You really think you can make up for the difference in numbers with this?"

Even if the other side proved to be more experienced, the pirates still had overwhelmingly superior numbers. No matter how many ships they lost, there would be more behind them to continue the attack on House Banfield's fleet.

The two sides clashed, and both fleets took damage to their front lines, yet none of the attacks reached Goaz's ship. His ship was equipped with an energy shield, and several vessels specialized for defense were arranged around his own, protecting him. There was nothing for him to fear from his enemy.

"Keep pushing—we've got the advantage! Crush them!"

They were putting up a bit of a fight, that was all. The pirates surged forward, bearing down on House Banfield's fleet.

The adjutant anticipated their foe's moves. "Normally, a noble's private army will start to flee right about now. Once one of them breaks rank and turns tail, they fall apart from there."

When one ship fled, the rest eventually followed, breaking up the fleet's formation. It was easier to run down a fleeing enemy, so the adjutant was hoping for that to happen.

"Well, they've got the balls not to run. If they want to fight so bad, we'll bring it to them."

"You got it, Boss."

Poorly trained crews belonging to nobility tended to flee as soon as they were at a disadvantage, either because of a lack of experience or because they simply lacked loyalty. However, so far House Banfield's fleet was sticking together and fighting in a show of perseverance. Figuring they'd pound the fight out of them eventually, the pirates continued their charge.

"I bet they'll run soon," Goaz said.

Finally, the movements of the House Banfield ships changed. Seeing this, the adjutant figured the clash was coming to an end. "We got 'em on the ropes, Boss."

"'Bout what I'd expect from 'em."

The two men believed their enemy was breaking formation, and that the battle was over.

However, something wasn't right.

How long's this battle gonna drag on for? Irritated, I rose from my chair and beckoned the commander over. He looked busy, but I didn't care.

"Hey, how long are we gonna run?"

"This is the best we can do at the moment, my lord. In order to win, we have to drag out the battle as long as we can while we wait for the regular army to—"

That's what your plan is? I shouldn't have left things to you guys.

"Wait for the regular army? Who ordered you to do that? I'm going to fight here and now, and win with my force alone. We'll finish this before the others even get here."

"B-but, my lord..."

"The enemy has greater numbers. What's going to happen if they send a detached force to my planet?"

"W-well...there's a possibility that our defensive unit won't be able to fend them off. That's why we have to keep them occupied here!"

"Don't be ridiculous! You want to just let them into my domain?"

I couldn't give a shit about my planet, really, but Amagi was there. *Well, and Brian.* There was no point in victory if my territory was torn apart and Amagi was dead. Actually, did I *really* not care what happened to my planet and my people? After all the work it had taken to build things up this far, having someone else tear it all down would be humiliating.

"We're going to crush them here. Don't let any of them

escape! I won't allow a single one of them to set foot on my planet!"

"B-but what about your own life, my lord?"

True, I did value my own life, but there was no point in prolonging this game of tag with the pirates. *Fighting against a more powerful enemy, you have to do everything you can to bring them down to your level. We're up against pirates; they're not afraid to play dirty. I don't want to give them any extra time to strategize.*

"Don't argue with me. Now then, I brought my own personal craft since it's my first battle and all. We'll have to get closer to the enemy for me to go out and fight them, right?"

Everyone was looking at me with harsh eyes, as if to say "What does this brat think he's doing, talking about matters he doesn't understand?" But I didn't care. Plus, if I waited for the regular army to intervene, they'd claim my treasure. *Goaz is* my *prey! I'm not giving him to anyone else!*

"All ships, charge."

At my order, the commander's eyes widened. "Wha—?"

"Did you not hear me? Charge with all ships, I said. Hurry up and do it. I'm going to deploy in the Avid, so just tell me when we're close enough. We'll be sending out the rest of the mobile knights too."

I was tired of sitting on the bridge, so I headed for the

hangar, where the Avid was stored. *Jeez, if you were just trying to keep them busy, you should have told me sooner. What a waste of time.*

On the bridge of Goaz's ship, he and his adjutant were becoming agitated. They'd realized something was odd when the firefight hadn't gone the way they'd expected. Normally, their enemy's attack would be waning by now, but they showed no signs of stopping.

Goaz bolted up from his chair. "What's going on?"

The screen in front of him magnified the distant enemy fleet. What he saw was the enemy ships retaining formation... Fighting, not fleeing. Seeing this, it was hard to imagine this fleet losing its will to fight.

His adjutant was just as surprised. "They're not retreating? No, it looks like they're tightening their formation and advancing!"

"Send out the mobile knights!" Goaz bellowed. "All the mercenaries too!"

They were close enough to send their humanoid weapons out to fight now, but they realized then that the enemy had already deployed their own mobile knights, and these were cutting into Goaz's front lines.

"This kid has got a backbone. I'm definitely gonna nab him so I can make him my toy."

For the first time, Goaz simmered with anger, finally acknowledging his enemy.

On the bridge, the commander barked out order after order. The staff officers were busy confirming the state of the battle and dishing out their own instructions. One officer—the one Liam had been talking with earlier— glanced at the lord's now-empty chair.

"I didn't think he'd really go out there."

All the other soldiers were bewildered as well. They'd boarded Liam's battleship in order to serve beside him, but then he'd deployed in a mobile knight. He'd ordered the charge, and now he was on the battlefield himself, leaving the commander and staff officers to oversee the chaotic bridge.

"Just move the mobile knights forward! Don't let our lord take fire!"

"He has pulled away from his guards and is rushing ahead!"

"We have to protect him, whatever it takes!"

The soldiers all looked up at the wall-length main monitor, watching the Avid's movements.

"So this is a knight..."

Knights were truly something special, unlike rank-and-file soldiers. They had trained their minds and bodies from a young age, and regular soldiers stood no chance against them. There was such a difference in their abilities that when they fought, all regular soldiers could do was try to surround and overwhelm them. Mobile knights piloted by regular soldiers and those piloted by knights moved in completely different ways, even if the machines had the same specs.

There were no knights in House Banfield. The only one in this domain with the abilities of a knight was Liam himself.

The monitor displayed the Avid, Liam within it, blasting through enemy forces with a rocket launcher in its right manipulator and a laser sword in its left. As soon as the pirates' mobile knights drew close, he cut through them with his laser blade, blasting holes in their battleships with his rocket launcher.

When the rocket launcher ran out of ammunition, he tossed it aside, summoned a glowing magic portal in front of the Avid, and pulled a new weapon from within. He had a massive supply of weapons at his disposal, all of which were stored with spatial magic. This was something only a high-class weapon like the Avid could pull off; mass-produced machines couldn't hope to achieve it. He maneuvered the Avid freely through space, displaying an overwhelming might.

House Banfield's fleet was still struggling with communications issues, but they could hear Liam's voice interspersed with static. *"Ah ha ha ha, just try to stop me!"*

As they watched Liam crush his enemies without hesitation, destroying pirate ship after pirate ship, one soldier wiped a tear from his cheek. "He's so strong. He really is a knight."

Since he hadn't had his coming-of-age ceremony yet, Liam was still considered a child, so these soldiers felt they were watching a child battle gleefully with pirates.

The commander approached his men, finished with dispensing orders for now. "Does he frighten you?"

Snapping to attention, one soldier uttered, "Oh, Commander. No, I..."

"At ease," said the commander, who then returned to his chair. While directing the battleship, he'd been stealing glances at the Avid on the monitors. "I wonder if our lord would have lived a normal childhood if he hadn't been born a noble. It's actually a shame."

On the main screen, Liam cackled as he slaughtered his foes. There were of course some troubling aspects to the sight, but overall, the morale of his fighters soared as they watched him slay his enemies. Only the commander watched Liam with some regret.

"A shame, you say? Even though he's so strong?" his colonel asked.

The commander nodded and shared the tale of Liam's past. "He was abandoned by his parents at a young age and saddled with a ruined territory on the outskirts of the Empire. Through his hard work, he managed to build up his domain, but now he's fighting with pirates to preserve it. To be honest, I'd like to know how to raise a child like this myself."

Revitalizing such a barren territory at his age was already a miracle, but the young lord was even fighting pirates on the front line of battle as a knight, displaying overwhelming strength.

"I'd like my own children to learn from him," the commander muttered to himself.

These former Imperial Army soldiers had been forced out to Liam's domain. Many of them were stubborn men, ousted for being too serious, too diligent, too upright. In other words, many of them were honest, hardworking people. This was because the Guide had wanted to gather people who would be the complete opposite of Liam, who aimed to become an evil lord.

"I've spent some time thinking about my life since being driven out here, and I've decided that I'm glad it happened. I never would've thought that this was how I'd meet the one lord I should be serving."

He'd known of the lord's administrative talents, but he had never imagined that Liam would be such a powerful knight as well. Liam truly shone in the soldiers' eyes. They were enchanted by the sight of him crushing all the enemies before him, cutting a path forward.

"So there truly are great rulers, skilled with both the pen and the blade. Who would've thought I'd witness a noble lord fighting as a knight on the front lines?" the commander mused aloud. "In him, I've seen a *real* noble for the first time. He was right when he said that if his domain were attacked while we waited for reinforcements, everything would be for naught. If our lord survives, House Banfield will be safe, but it's for the sake of his people that he wishes to defeat the pirates."

As he fought, Liam personified the ideal knight. Seeing the mettle of this noble, who normally should have been sitting safely in the rear, as he protected his own territory from harm, made his soldiers ashamed of their cowardly initial strategy.

"Did he really have to go and fight himself, though?" the colonel asked.

"House Banfield has no knights, so it was necessary. It's true that this is shameful, but who could be a more dependable fighter? He vowed not to let even one pirate set foot on his land."

Liam was fighting on the front lines to defend his people—at least, that was what it looked like to the soldiers. This young noble had thrown away a safer, more drawn-out strategy in favor of a quick, decisive battle, all for the sake of his subjects.

"This is the first time I've actually seen a noble *protecting* his people. It's rare to even see them fight at all. It's true that it's the best thing he can do for his domain, but he's risking his life for his people!"

It just seemed wrong for the person in charge to be fighting in the vanguard, but he gave his troops the sense that they could win if they fought alongside him. Nowadays, nobles never stepped forward like this, even if they had the power of knights at their disposal. Most nobles who improved their own abilities only did so with the thought of seeming superior and exploiting others. This was the current state of Imperial nobility. There were very few nobles of decent character, and those who did exist were not nearly as resolute as Liam. Today, Liam had proven himself to be a true rarity in the Empire.

"You weaklings are nothing but prey! At least try *to entertain me!"*

Perhaps he was enjoying the battlefield a little more than was necessary, but that was no doubt better than shedding tears as he fought.

Their lord was laughing as he faced down the pirates, and his men felt less anxious as they watched him.

10 Successor—
ORIGINATOR OF THE WAY OF THE FLASH

"I'M INVINCIBLE!"

Inside the Avid's cockpit, I couldn't stop laughing as I worked the control sticks.

This is it—this is what I wanted! I have enough power to bend my enemy to my will. I can destroy my foes with the weapon that I spent so much damn money on.

I was up against pirates, a terrifying foe that reminded me of the debt collectors I had feared in my past life, and I was vanquishing them with my own strength. It was intoxicating. I had finally crossed over from the side of the victim to that of the victimizer. This thought filled my heart.

"C'mon, c'mon! Keep 'em comin'!"

The Avid moved exactly as I commanded in the weightless environment of space. Its black, heavily armored frame boasted two large shields on its shoulders.

Not only were they physical barriers, but they also contained technology that repelled laser beams and magic. Because of them, I could fight without too much concern for defense. Then there were the Avid's other specs. As restored by the Seventh Weapons Factory, the Avid had more power than any common mobile knight. Incredibly sturdy and responding perfectly to my piloting, it was the best craft I could have asked for.

"Good, Avid! You're the best there is! Now, crush our enemy!"

I bisected an enemy with my laser blade.

"You're so strong! You're a powerhouse, Avid!"

I was thrilled at how powerful the Avid had proven to be, and I was eternally thankful for Master Yasushi's wise teachings. One training session in particular came to mind. I was supposed to be learning swordsmanship, yet Master had urged me into a weightless chamber where I dodged projectiles while blindfolded. At the time, I'd thought, *What use is this gonna be?* Now I felt embarrassed for wondering. Master's teachings were coming in plenty useful—not just for sword fighting, but for piloting as well. He must have known that I would be fighting battles like this, so he'd honed my skills for piloting from a young age. There had been meaning in each and every one of his lessons!

"I really had a great master, didn't I?"

I ran out of ammo for the bazooka in my right hand, so I chucked it away. A pirate's mobile knight charged me, but I grabbed it with the Avid's manipulator and crushed its head.

My craft was on a completely different level than the mobile knights the pirates were using. They were practically toys compared to my Avid. It was like a tiny kei car racing a sports car.

I manifested the magic circle near the craft's empty right hand and drew a new bazooka from it. The Avid stood out from all my other mobile knights floating about it, so the pirates crowded around me. *Well, I've got no shortage of enemies.*

"Aw, you came all this way just to let me kill you? Thanks!"

I couldn't help smirking. When I pulled the trigger on a control stick, several large magic circles formed around the Avid. Multiple weapons I'd stored with spatial magic appeared from the circles, box-like shapes that poked out and locked on to the enemy. These boxes were missile pods, loaded with thousands of missiles. The pirates who noticed this hurriedly turned their backs and tried to flee, but they were too slow.

"You're just a *little* too late."

Missile after missile fired from the pods and chased after my fleeing enemies. When they reached their targets, they exploded, obliterating all the mobile knights they struck.

"Fear me! Tremble in terror! Let your pitiful deaths spread the name of Liam Sera Banfield through the galaxy!"

A number of the pirates' mobile knights managed to escape the sea of explosions. Their maneuvers were different from the others, so I figured they were piloted by knights.

"Pirate knights, eh?"

This was what people called knights who'd stooped to a life of piracy. Many of them became mercenaries or took leadership roles among pirate armadas. Knights played an especially important role in pirates' offensive strategies.

The knights spread out behind, above, and below me—challenging me to a three-dimensional battle only possible in space. They attacked the Avid, but their beams couldn't penetrate the shields mounted on my craft's shoulders. An energy field made up of sparkling particles of light enveloped the Avid in a sphere and blocked every single one of their attacks. Even when they tried physical ammunition, their rounds couldn't pierce the Avid's armor.

"Whoa! This thing can't be beat!"

The pirate knights switched to close-range weapons, like blades, and moved in. I had to dodge these attacks since even the Avid wouldn't be unscathed if a knight's blade reached it. It kinda felt as if they were trying to scratch up a new car of mine, so I tried to avoid being grazed by their blades. *Nobody likes getting nicks on something they just bought, do they?*

I tossed my bazooka and took out a rifle, but the knights moved in a completely different way than the enemies I'd been fighting until now, easily dodging my shots.

"These guys are definitely not normal pirates, but still... not good enough!"

One enemy got in too close, and when I passed by him with the Avid, his craft was cut in two.

"You respond to me perfectly, Avid!"

Even though the Avid was difficult to handle, it could keep up with my reaction speed and proved the perfect partner. As the pirates' mobile knights came at me, I cut them down one by one. I slashed up, brought my blade down, swept it diagonally, hoisted horizontally. Each time I swung my blade, an enemy was sliced through, then exploded.

One of the knights rushed the Avid and challenged me to a contest of strength, catching my blade with his own. When we made contact, I picked up his voice on the com.

"What did you just do? What school are you using?"

Since studying swordsmanship and multiple other fighting techniques was a core part of being a knight, they either belonged to a school or had studied at one in the past.

This was the craft that had moved the best out of all the pirates' mobile knights. Finding myself curious about him as well, I decided to indulge him. *Well, it's something I can do since I don't feel particularly threatened by him. I'm the stronger one here, so I have the privilege of showing him just how relaxed I am.*

"It's the Way of the Flash. You haven't heard of it? I was taught by Yasushi."

"Of course I haven't! You're pretty cocky for a guy who uses some super obscure style! I've never even heard of your teacher either!"

That pissed me off, so I tossed the rifle in my right hand and crushed the pirate knight's head instead.

"'Super obscure'? Fine! I'll just crush all of you and make the Way of the Flash famous myself!"

Having lost interest, I let go of the pirate knight and thrust my blade through its cockpit. I then sought a new victim, sending the Avid toward a nearby pirate ship.

As my boosters spewed flames, rays of light shot after the speeding Avid. Racing through the hail of beam attacks, I charged at the pirate ship and stabbed my blade into its hull. The ship exploded.

"Now where can I find my next prey?"

On his main screen, Goaz watched the black mobile knight that flew unscathed through beams and explosions.

"Wh-what is that thing? Who's the knight piloting it?"

He thought for sure it was a named knight, one who was particularly renowned. When the craft had first appeared, he'd believed it was just a large, old-fashioned unit, and they were thrusting every chess piece they had onto the board. But the craft had cut through all his pirate knights without even giving them a chance to defend themselves.

Goaz had broken out into a cold sweat, so afraid had he become of the black mobile knight.

"What is such an accomplished knight doing out here?"

He was panicking now, thinking that his enemies had an expert fighter on their side, but his adjutant received a report that shocked him.

"Boss! It's the head of House Banfield who's piloting that mobile knight! That's Liam Sera Banfield himself!"

"What?!" Goaz began trembling with rage. "Those mercenaries I paid good money for lost to one little brat? The mobile knights I supplied them with weren't cheap either!"

Goaz had paid a substantial amount to hire those pirate knights, and he'd outfitted them with mobile knights from another nation's army, bought through the black market. He'd changed how the machines looked, but they should have performed much better than the crafts used by his other pirates. He couldn't believe they hadn't even put up a fight against Liam.

"Well, if their boss is out there, good. Surround him and give him all we've got! This idiot really is a kid, jumping into the fray just to make a name for himself."

With his lackeys watching, Goaz had to maintain a brave face. Being a pirate himself, he knew pirates were the least trustworthy bunch out there, betraying one another at the drop of a hat. The more of them you gathered, the more traitorous types you'd have. If his men thought they couldn't win this battle, it was quite possible they'd betray him.

As he sat in his chair projecting confidence, Goaz

watched his fighters obey his order and crowd around Liam's craft.

Then his jaw dropped. "Wha—?!"

All the mobile knights crowding around Liam had been struck down in a single instant. As soon as they'd gotten somewhat close, they'd exploded. Pirate ships had been cut in half too. It was like a bad dream.

Th-this can't be happening! I know knights are strong, but this is beyond that. What is he? What is this guy? He couldn't believe what he was seeing.

Just like that, Liam started heading straight for Goaz's flagship. He plunged through a crowd of pirate ships, and as his clamoring enemies tried to shoot him down, they ended up firing on one another.

"Those idiots! Tell them to stop! Take him out with mobile knights!"

The pirates were panicking over a single opponent—but Liam was not their only enemy.

"Boss!" Goaz's adjutant shouted. "The enemy's charging us!"

The enemy fleet was pressing forward, following Liam in a cone-shaped formation. They pierced through the unorganized pirate forces and made their way toward Goaz. The highly trained troops guided the ships in perfect formation, and the ragtag bunch of pirates didn't stand a chance against them. All their expensive equipment didn't amount to much under failed management.

Goaz slammed his fist down on his armrest. "Those useless idiots!"

There were a lot of former soldiers in Goaz's gang, but most of them hadn't been through proper military training. These weaker pirates were the first to fumble.

Having lost his advantage, Goaz attempted to strategize. *Things are going poorly now. If I'm gonna lose, I should just get outta here and lie low for a while. I was thinkin' this group was gettin' a little too big, anyway.*

It was tempting to be the leader of a huge pirate armada, but he was becoming tired of the responsibility. Deciding to throw it all away, Goaz called his adjutant over and whispered in his ear.

"We're gonna run. Just tell those we can trust and leave the rest behind."

The adjutant was surprised, but nodded nonetheless. "Gotcha, Boss."

With that, Goaz's flagship and its guard ships went on the move.

After I get away, I'll send some assassins after the kid. I can start over as many times as I want. I've still got this, after all. He squeezed the alchemy box in his hand.

"Come on!" his adjutant shouted. "Let's get out of here!"

"We can't!" the pirate piloting the ship responded. "Our allies are in the way!"

The adjutant punched the man in the face. "Then destroy them! Hurry up! The enemy's right in front of us!"

Normally, it would be unthinkable for the adjutant to act in this manner, even if they were at a disadvantage and needed to retreat. He was just that afraid of Liam, who was rapidly closing the distance between them. All the pirates were terrified of the unrelenting lord.

"Got you."

The moment after they heard Liam's voice, the pirate ship lurched. Goaz and his men went pale as they gaped at the monitor, which showed Liam's Avid standing on their hull. The mobile knight then began taking out all of the ship's guns.

"How's an old hunk of junk like that so *strong*?" Goaz hollered as he fled the bridge of his ship.

I reached the enemy flagship, which was attempting to flee, and alighted on it. Standing on its hull gave the other ships ample opportunity to attack me, but none of them did.

"Guess even pirates won't attack their captain's ship."

As the pirates hesitated, I walked the Avid boldly over the ship.

"Escape pods would probably come from...there?"

I took some shots with my rifle, sealing up their escape route, and shot down some fleeing pirates.

"It's too late for you to run away now. I'm gonna teach you exactly who you tried to mess with. Then your treasure's gonna be mine!"

As I disabled this ship's capabilities, the other ships around it tried running, but my allies had finally caught up. They confirmed my safety through communications, though with heavy interference.

"Are you safe, my lord?"

"All good here. Leave a thousand of our ships here and follow those fleeing pirates with the rest. Don't let them get away, you hear me? And don't accept their surrender either—we're crushing every last one of them!"

"Yes, sir!"

My fleet pursued the escaping pirates. In any world, you take the most damage in war during retreat.

One of my ships pulled up along the flagship, and its fighters prepared to board. I wrenched open a hatch to get into the hangar. A mobile knight was waiting for me inside. It shot me with a rocket launcher, but that wasn't enough to destroy the Avid. The explosion enveloped my craft, yet the cockpit didn't so much as shudder.

"Aww, you got the Avid dirty."

Seeing the Avid almost completely unharmed, some pirates within the hangar, outfitted in space suits, panicked and fired at me with rifles.

"Outta my way."

Lasers had been installed all over the Avid and blew the pirates away. I cut down the mobile knight, and when there was no one left to oppose me, I donned a helmet. My pilot outfit itself was a powered suit designed for battle. I equipped a blade to my belt and hopped out of the Avid with a rifle in hand, boarding the pirate ship.

"Now, I'd say it's time for a treasure hunt."

Small crafts dispersed from my fleet were flooding into the hangar. My troops poured out of them and gathered before me, assembling into a row. These soldiers, taller than me and also clad in battle-ready gear, formed an intimidating force. I was delighted that they all showed me the utmost respect. *There's nothing more important than social standing. Look at all these adults saluting a kid like me.*

"We've come to escort you back, Lord Liam."

They seem to have the wrong idea about why they're here, though. This is the fun part, guys!

"Wrong. It's time for the treasure hunt to begin. You're coming with me."

Hearing this, the soldiers raised their voices in protest.

"It's too dangerous, my lord! We've taken control of the nuclear reactor, but the enemy could still launch a suicide attack—"

"You think an enemy cowardly enough to flee would blow themselves up? Come on, let's go."

I headed deeper into the ship with my reluctant troops. All the soldiers' powered suits were more rugged than mine, and they bunched up around me as a living shield.

Their artificial gravity had been disabled or something, so loose objects floated in the halls as we moved through them. The soldiers around me pushed them aside to clear my path as I marched forward. Though there was no gravity, the soles of my powered suit magnetized to the floor, enabling me to walk with no issues.

"It's cleaner than I thought it'd be for a pirate ship. I figured it'd be more squalid in here."

The commanding officer of the boarding party was still freaking out about every little thing I did.

"Lord Liam, please don't get too far ahead of us!"

As I was surging forward, and getting plenty of complaints, I sensed danger and ordered everyone to stop.

"Someone's hiding... There!"

Around the corner, I could feel several people lying in wait for us. There were others hiding in the ceiling as well, so I directed my soldiers to shoot them. They pointed their rifles at the ceiling and riddled it with holes. Airborne beads of red blood floated out from the openings, so I assumed we'd gotten them.

One of my men reported, "They were wearing suits that don't show up on sensors. I can't imagine how pirates got their hands on such expensive equipment, though."

Their gear was indeed pricey, and that told me I could expect some sweet treasure from them.

"Rich pirates, eh? Well, that's to our advantage now. Come on, let's go."

I had my boarding force take care of the pirates around the corner, and then we all continued on, eventually arriving at a spacious room. Several pirate knights in powered suits awaited us there.

"How careless of you!"

I rolled my eyes as the pirate knight shouted out his taunt during what was supposed to be an ambush. Master had never revealed his location before launching surprise attacks on me. *These knights are second rate.* There was no need to even worry when they attacked us.

"Protect Lord Liam!"

My men, however, were in a fluster. They tried to get in front of me, but I brushed them aside.

"There's no need." I walked forward, ignoring the pirate knights. My men were confused, so I turned around and asked them, "What are you doing? Hurry up."

"Huh? But—"

The backward momentum of the attacking pirate knights carried them to the floor and walls, where their bodies splattered apart into chunks.

"Lord Liam, what did you just do?"

"I cut them."

My soldiers hadn't even been able to detect my slashes. I took some pride in the improvement of my skills, but it didn't make me very happy to cut down second-rate pirate knights. Master would probably scold me if I boasted about something like that.

I'm still so far from his level. Just when will I catch up to Master Yasushi? I still vividly remembered his slashes, how I couldn't even tell that he'd drawn his sword from its scabbard. I felt like I was still just a child playing copycat.

Of course, in current company, my skills seemed remarkable. My men followed me in awed silence, most likely afraid.

That's right, fear me! Fear your master, and worship him!

The soldiers who'd boarded watched Liam as he walked in front of them. He was wearing a powered suit, which made him appear a little larger, but his immature body was still undeniably slight. Though surrounded by adults, his presence was of the greatest among them. There was almost something grand about his small frame.

"He's completely at ease facing so many enemies."

Normally, common soldiers cursed their bad luck if they ran into a knight, but thanked their fortune if they had a formidable knight on their side. This was how great the difference was for them now.

One of the soldiers expressed his admiration for Liam. "His school granted him full mastery even though he wasn't even an adult yet. Is our lord actually superhuman?"

Liam had long held a reputation for mastery of political management, but no one had ever spoken of his military might. This was only natural. Since he hadn't reached adulthood yet, he had never undergone formal military training. How was anyone to know of his talents in that area? Of course, now that he'd proven himself in the field, word of his abilities would spread like wildfire.

"His strength is unbelievable. We're serving someone truly incredible."

The soldiers of House Banfield had never been outside of their domain, so they had no idea just how remarkable Liam was. The only people they had to compare him to were his last two predecessors, and compared to them, Liam was entirely too perfect. Witnessing their lord in battle today, he came out looking even more amazing than they'd already thought he was.

"He took out those pirate knights like they were nothing. He's got full mastery in some unique swordsmanship discipline, doesn't he?"

A soldier muttered to his compatriot, "I think it's called the Way of the Flash? There must be some incredible sword schools out there."

11 Treasure

T HE PIRATES on the flagship ran around in consternation. Some of their knights were still putting up a fight, but most of them were outnumbered and taken down by the enemy. Even knights had their limits when surrounded by trained soldiers.

In the first place, the most skilled pirate knights had already deployed, and the only ones left were those who hadn't wanted to go out and fight. They didn't have any real strength, so they were taken out all too quickly when they were overrun by Liam's soldiers.

With its training and the quality of its equipment, House Banfield's private army operated as if it were the Empire's regular army.

Goaz's adjutant cursed as he fled through the ship. "Damn you, Goaz! How dare he run on his own!"

He'd ordered his lackeys to deal with the boarding force and then up and vanished. The adjutant had now abandoned the bridge himself and was frantically trying to come up with some way to get out of this situation.

He stopped and hid around a corner to check a terminal and find out what was going on in the ship. "Shit! We're sealed tight; there's no way off the ship! Dammit! I don't want to die here."

As he fell to his knees, an enemy squad led by a sword-wielding knight spotted him. He bolted upright and tried to sprint away, but no matter which way he turned, enemies were all around him. Finally, the adjutant held up both hands in surrender.

"W-wait! Please, just hear me out!"

The small knight, sword resting on his shoulder, stopped and commanded his subordinates not to shoot. From his voice, he seemed to be quite a young knight.

This is my chance. I don't care if I have to cry and beg him—I'm going to find a way to stay alive.

"I-I was just being used by Goaz. Please, let me go."

This knight wore a full-face helmet, so the adjutant couldn't see his expression.

"I know! I can tell you where the treasure is. I can't open the lock for you, but I can at least take you to it, so let me live... Please!"

The adjutant got down on hands and knees, but the knight said nothing. One of his subordinates, however, tapped away at a tablet and reported, "Lord Liam, it appears this man is the Goaz Pirate Gang's second-in-command. I highly doubt someone in such a high position was just being used."

Hearing the name Liam, the adjutant raised his head. "Liam? *You're*—I mean, of course you are, your lordship. When I first saw you, I thought you had the air of a ruler about you. What would you say to hiring me, my lord? Think about it. As a commander of the Goaz Pirate Gang, I could surely provide you with...with..."

Suddenly, the view in front of him changed. His body hadn't moved at all, but his field of vision was spinning terribly. In zero gravity, he saw his own body... without its head.

"Huh?" was the last thing the adjutant thought.

As he watched the battle, the Guide was speechless. He stood in space atop a destroyed pirate ship.

"This is impossible. What *is* that? What is that power?!" He was bewildered by Liam's strength. No swordsmanship school named the Way of the Flash existed in this world; it was just a lie Yasushi had made up. And yet, Liam had unknowingly created it himself.

"Even if he did develop some talent, what the heck is that power he's using? What did that man teach him?" During the time the Guide hadn't been monitoring him, Liam had grown stronger than he could have ever imagined. This was a battle that Liam should never have been able to win.

The Guide held his head with both hands, completely baffled by the power Liam had obtained. "It hurts... My chest burns... Dammit!"

Horrible feelings of gratitude and trust continued to flow into him from Liam. He could hardly stomach them.

"I can't be picky about how I do this anymore. Goaz, congratulations on your new special power." He waved his arm, producing a small cloud of black smoke. "This goes against the way I do things, but I have no choice now. This is all your fault, Liam. Honestly, you've caused me nothing but grief."

Considering the Guide's hand in all this, it was a rather ironic comment.

Goaz hid inside his ship, clutching the alchemy box to

his chest. All he could hear were the screams of his crew, each one jolting him to the core.

"No! I don't wanna die, I don't wanna die, I don't wanna die! Not in a place like this!"

This man, captain of a pirate gang, had inflicted incredible suffering on others, yet now he was sobbing in fright. His huge body was curled up, knees at his chest, as he quivered and chewed away at a thumbnail.

The whole source of Goaz's strength was the vast wealth granted to him by the alchemy box. As a fighter, he might have been a little stronger than average, but he was no knight. If armed soldiers discovered him, he'd be killed in the blink of an eye.

"Sh-should I beg for my life? N-no, they'll just turn me in for my bounty. I-I know—if I offer them treasure that I make with this..."

If Goaz had put the alchemy box to better use, he could have made a vast fortune and wouldn't even have needed to become a pirate. He'd only ended up in this situation because he'd spent his life pillaging. It was his own fault. Of course, no one could have predicted that he'd lose to Liam.

As Goaz sat there, black smoke began to envelop him.

"Wh-what the—?"

He heard a voice in his ear—the voice of the Guide. "Don't waste this chance I'm giving you, Goaz..."

"Wh-wh-who's there?" he stammered, and the smoke poured into his mouth.

At that moment, the Guide revealed himself, and Goaz gripped his own throat as he writhed in pain. He dropped the alchemy box, but he had no time to worry about that.

"Whomever you'd like. Just know I'm giving you a chance to kill Liam. Or do you *want* to lose?"

Goaz shook his head, and the Guide flashed his crescent-moon smile.

"Good."

Finally freed from the pain of inhaling the black smoke, Goaz released his throat and looked down at his hand. It was the same hand he was used to seeing, but the color was wrong.

"What's this? I'm feeling stronger and stronger... I'm not afraid anymore! I have *nothing* to fear! I'm strong... I'm strooong!"

His initial shock at seeing his bluish-black flesh was gone. In its place were surges of confidence and power. All fear forgotten, Goaz twisted his face into an ugly grin.

The Guide looked pleased as well. "Your skin is as hard as adamantite now. You've surpassed humanity, and nothing can stop you. Now, go!"

"You braaat! It's *really* gonna hurt when I kill youuu!"

The Guide watched Goaz run off and put a hand to his forehead. "I pushed myself a little hard there. Maybe that was a bit too mischievous." He felt fatigued from all the times he'd used the door between worlds and manipulated things lately.

"No matter how strong Liam is, he'll no longer be able to cut Goaz. I hope he regrets boarding this ship in his arrogance."

When the Guide had departed, a small light floated over to the forgotten alchemy box. It was the same one that had snuck into the Avid, keeping watch over the Guide all this time. The light transformed into a dog with black-and-brown fur, then ran down the hall toward Liam.

As I walked through the ship's halls, I felt a familiar presence. I glanced in the direction I'd sensed it and found that the presence wasn't human. I only caught a glimpse of something rushing by, but I could make out a brown tail—the tail of a dog.

"Huh?"

"Is something the matter, Lord Liam?" one of my men asked me.

"Ah... Was there a dog over there just now?"

"A dog? No, there are no life signs around us, and there couldn't be a dog here anyway. I can't imagine they'd have a zero-gravity suit for a dog too."

Had I been mistaken? After some thought, it dawned on me why the sight had seemed so familiar. It had to be my dog from my previous life. Even though he hadn't come to meet me on my deathbed, he had still been incredibly important to me. And yet, I'd somehow forgotten about him after reincarnating into this world.

"I can't believe I forgot about you." *I guess I can't blame him for not showing up. It's fine, though—I don't want him to see how I am now.* He was one of my few true friends in my past life who had never betrayed me.

While I was musing, a soldier got my attention. "Is something wrong?"

"No, it's nothing. Anyway, let's take a look over there."

I went in the direction where I thought I'd seen the tail. This passageway wasn't clean like the others, being full of junk. It looked like it was probably used as a storage space. There were plenty of places to hide, so my men moved through it carefully, but I didn't sense anyone inside. I was a little disappointed, in fact, since there was no dog either. I had planned on rescuing it if I really did find one.

I sighed and looked down, then spotted something at my feet. "What's this?"

It was a golden box, small enough to hold in one hand. I picked it up to take a closer look. It bore all sorts of patterns and ornamentation, so I felt like I might have stumbled across a good find.

"Hey, this looks nice. I think I'll keep it."

One of my men gave me a rather uncharitable look. "So it's true that you're fond of gold, Lord Liam."

"What's wrong with gold? I love it."

"What about mithril and adamantite?"

"Hm? Sure, I like those too, but for me, gold is best."

I don't like those exasperated looks my men are giving me, but mithril is silver, right? I think adamantite is just something you make weapons out of. Sure, they're valuable, but the value in those things is in how you use them.

While I was examining the box, I once again saw the tail out of the corner of my eye.

"Again..."

"Lord Liam, please don't get ahead of us!"

I left my men behind and chased after the dog, but I arrived at a dead end. There was something about this wall that bothered me, though. When I touched it, I discovered a hidden door.

"I didn't find the dog, but I smell treasure! There's a secret door here, boys!"

I had my men destroy the hidden door, and when I stepped through it, I was indeed greeted by a mountain of treasure. However, it wasn't the gold and silver I'd been expecting. Instead, the room was filled with curios and antiques.

"No luck, eh?" I was disappointed, but my men were surprised and delighted.

"N-no, this is great luck, my lord! These all look expensive!"

"I'm sure they're all fakes. Like this box thing. It's just a fake, right?"

"Th-there's no way to tell without appraising them."

"Whatever. Okay, let's take it home at least. Man, this is so disappointing."

All the curios that House Banfield had previously owned had proved to be fakes, so I simply assumed the majority of these would be the same. Still, I rummaged through the items to see what I could find, and I stumbled upon a sword.

"Oh, here's something interesting at least."

It looked very old, and like something you'd find in a fantasy game—especially the design of its hilt and scabbard. It wasn't too flashy, but the blade had a nice look to it when I unsheathed it. Appreciating how the light shined off of it, I felt sort of strange. I'd thought everything in the room was a forgery, but this seemed perfectly usable, which put me in a good mood.

"All right, I like it. I think I'll use this."

"Maybe you shouldn't," said one soldier. Clearly, he thought it would be a waste to put this antique into action. "It seems like it might be worth a lot."

"Sheesh," I muttered. "Weapons only have meaning if you use them. It's not like I bought it—I stole it from pirates, who stole it first."

I slipped the gold box into a large pocket in the back of my suit, handed my rifle and blade over to one of my men, and took up the old sword. *Now that the battle is all but over, I don't need other weapons. This sword's enough for me.*

"Now, where should we head ne—"

"Lord Liam, emergency transmission!" one of my men shouted.

Looks like my treasure hunt is over.

One of the teams from the boarding force had found Goaz, but he was sending soldiers in powered suits flying with just one arm. His skin was glossy and black.

"Dammit! Our bullets just bounce off him!"

"Beam weapons don't work either!"

"Fall back!"

One of the soldiers raised a rocket launcher and fired it at Goaz, but he emerged from the explosion and the smoke like nothing had happened. The soldiers paled.

Goaz rolled his neck, and his eyes shone red. "How dare you make a mess of my ship. Don't any of you think you're going home safe."

He was drunk with the power he'd obtained—the intoxicating feeling that he could do anything. In his mind, not even the strongest knight could defeat him now. He clenched his fist and it made a sound like no human hand should: metal scraping against metal.

"I'll make you all my toys!"

Goaz blew away the soldiers with the strength gifted to him by the Guide. Bullets, lasers, and explosives were all meaningless against him. One of the more quick-witted soldiers manipulated the air pressure in the corridor, but even that had no effect.

"What did this guy do to himself?!"

"Is he a cyborg?"

They tried to run, but he caught up in a flash. He grabbed them and hurled them through the air, making a show of his might. These highly trained soldiers were no match for him.

"Bring the boy! I'll take him down myself!"

One of the soldiers ordered the men around him, "Get Lord Liam off the ship! Do not let this thing find him!"

The soldiers kept attacking Goaz even though they knew it wouldn't have any effect, and Goaz continued tearing through them.

"What's wrong? That all you got?" Goaz punched a man so hard, he crushed the soldier's head, helmet and all, and then threw him aside. The man's body was bent in an unnatural way. He used one man as a shield and the gunfire stopped.

"This time, I'm gonna—" He threw aside the soldier he'd been using as a shield and took a step forward, but a wound suddenly appeared inside his body. "Wh-what?"

Goaz looked down at himself and found that he had several wounds. While he was trying to figure out what had happened to him, a person dropped down from above.

The man landed and slowly stood, gazing down at the badly chipped blade in his hand. "You're way too hard." He sounded amused.

Goaz couldn't see a face inside the figure's helmet, but he could picture a boy smiling. He reached out to try to grab his assailant, but something dropped to the ground. After a beat, he realized it was his own arm. Everything from the elbow down was gone.

"Huh?" While he stood there in shock, the boy in front of him tossed aside the damaged sword he'd been using. He had another sword in his hand now, which Goaz recalled seeing somewhere before. It was a very valuable weapon that he'd stored away in a secret room with the rest of his booty. It was the second most valuable thing among Goaz's treasures, after the alchemy box.

"H-hey, that's mine!"

The boy just smiled. "Oh, this? It's mine now. More importantly, you seem to have been quite busy." He rested the sword on his shoulder.

Goaz reached out to him once more. This time, his other arm dropped.

"Ngh!" Goaz couldn't even tell what was happening. All he knew was the boy had drawn the antique sword from its scabbard at some point.

This time, the knight looked down at the sword, impressed. "That's pretty amazing—not a single nick in the blade. I like it."

Goaz was armless now. While he stood frozen in confusion, black smoke spewed from the stumps of his arms and solidified into tentacles of flesh. In seconds, he had

something like whips for arms. Before he knew it, he was charging forward to attack.

"H-how dare youuu!"

But the boy just ignored him. "This is nice. I think this'll be my main weapon from now on."

The fleshy whips that Goaz rained down on the boy were shredded, and this time, one of his legs was cut off as well. He fell to one knee and more black smoke billowed out of his body.

"Aaargh..." Goaz trembled, all his confidence from earlier gone without a trace. As black blood spilled from him, his enemies banded together to protect the small knight.

"Lord Liam!"

When he heard that name, Goaz raised his head. He looked up at the boy before him, face twisting into a demonic expression.

"You! *You're* Liam!"

Liam was still so absorbed in his new sword that he wasn't even looking at Goaz. "That's right, I'm Liam. But that's 'Lord Liam' to you, scum. Who is this jet-black guy, anyway? Is he some kinda cyborg or something?"

One of his men offered a hesitant answer. "The color of his skin has changed, but I believe this is Goaz."

"This guy?"

Just then, a sharp horn began growing out of Goaz's severed left arm. "Don't ignore meee!" He thrust it forth, trying to pierce Liam's heart, and this time, everything below his shoulder was lopped off.

Liam looked down at Goaz, who was now kneeling one ground. He rested his sword on his shoulder again and stared at Goaz's face. "So you're Goaz?"

Goaz trembled more violently now, absolutely terrified of the boy before him. *What is he? What the hell is he? How can he cut me when bullets bounce right off of me? I don't get it! It makes no sense!*

The stupefied Goaz begged Liam for his life. "Please... Let me go."

"Hm? What was that?"

"I'll never defy you again. I-if you let me go, I'll give you an amazing treasure. So please... Just let me live!"

Liam laughed at Goaz's proposal. "I don't think so."

I'M THE EVIL LORD OF AN
INTERGALACTIC
EMPIRE

12 The Princess Knight

"I DON'T THINK SO." I smiled down at Goaz.

Goaz just looked up at me blankly for a second. "Huh? Er..."

"I said no."

A huge man with a terrifying face was groveling before me, trembling in fear. The sight was truly hilarious. With his ridiculously bulky muscles and tattoos—whether they were for fashion or intimidation, I didn't know—he reminded me of the debt collectors I'd feared in my past life. Frankly, it pissed me off just looking at him, but I was also very much enjoying holding his life in my hands and rejecting his pleas for mercy.

Man, I really am a monster, aren't I? Well, there's no point in going back to being a good person at this point.

Goaz once again pleaded for his life. "Please! I'll do anything, just spare me!"

The troops closest to me surrounded Goaz with their guns trained on him while the rest of them carried away our injured and dead. My men looked down at Goaz with ice-cold eyes. I could practically hear them thinking, *After all this, he's begging for his life?*

A captain of a huge pirate gang was crying and pleading for mercy before a person who looked like a child. The power of violence really was something. Well, I had my reasons for not granting his request, one being that he was just the type of predatory bully that had always pissed me off in my previous life, but he was also operating under a fundamental misunderstanding.

"There's something you're not getting here. You say that you'll do anything and that you'll give me an amazing treasure? Your treasure is already mine, and the only thing you can do for me now is become an entry on my list of achievements and get handed over to the Empire for the bounty on your head."

Goaz's eyes widened in shock, but to me there were no surprises here. There was nothing he could provide me that would be more valuable than the bounty I'd receive for turning him in to the Empire.

"Wait! I promise I'll be useful to you if you let me live! I-I may have lost, but you saw how strong I was, right? Those soldiers couldn't even scratch me! You could have a guy like that working for *you*. So please, don't do this! I've got a hidden treasure that's worth way more than the bounty on me! I'll give you the goods I have stashed in other places too!"

It probably wasn't all lies, but I was sure he was making up some of it just to get out of this situation. I was certain this guy would betray me if I let him live. Having seen plenty of people like him in my last life, I had decided never to trust anyone of his ilk again.

"What, you're still hiding more? You can tell it to an Imperial interrogator, then. I'm sure they'll employ plenty of fun and exciting techniques to get the information out of you so they can claim that treasure for themselves."

I sure didn't want to know what sort of things they'd do in that investigation, but Goaz would inevitably endure questioning and then execution. There would be no allowances for "extenuating circumstances" for this guy.

Finally realizing that there was no salvation in store for him, Goaz stopped pleading with me. "D-don't screw with me, you braaat!"

"Showing your true colors now? Why don't you be a little more cooperative?"

Somehow Goaz managed to stand, despite having only one foot. He lumbered toward me, black smoke spewing out of him.

I pointed my blade at him and coolly said, "Settle down." I slashed at him some more, just enough not to kill him, and severed his last limb while I was at it.

Goaz slid to the floor, looking like he had no idea what had just happened. After a moment, the reality finally registered, and he began to cry and beg for his life all over again.

"P-please, let me go! I'm begging you! Spare me! I don't want to die!"

I ignored him. They were all lines I was tired of hearing. Instead, I gazed at the sword I'd found, quite pleased. It seemed it would be even more useful than I'd thought. I had no more interest in Goaz, but one of my men asked me about his fate.

"You're really going to take him alive, Lord Liam?"

"Is there some problem with that?"

"N-no, it's just...he killed so many of my men."

All the soldiers around him seemed consumed by their hatred for Goaz as well. It was only natural, seeing as he'd killed their friends.

I don't like them questioning my methods, but these guys are basically just a machine that generates violence, so I don't want them holding a grudge against me either. Guess I should tread carefully with them. Not that I intend to change my decision, of course.

"It's my understanding that the bounty is higher if we hand him over alive, so that's what we're going to do." Or so I thought I'd heard.

"No, there's no difference in the bounty for a criminal as vicious as Goaz. In fact, they might reward you more if you can prove you saved them the trouble and finished him off."

The soldier who'd spoken brought up a holographic screen and displayed the information about Goaz's bounty, and it did indeed say something to that effect. *Guess I was mistaken. Well, that's embarrassing.*

"Aah, really?"

I glanced back at Goaz. He was still whimpering.

I can't believe this guy is the captain of a huge pirate gang that's destroyed entire planets. How pathetic. There's not a single molecule of me that wants to keep him alive.

I recalled a phrase I'd heard in my past life: "Debt collectors are human too." Who had said something so idiotic? Those leeches sucked every last drop out of me in my former life. They didn't have a speck of humanity in them; no amount of crying or appealing for relief had moved them at all. I'd lost all hope because of them, desperately asking myself, "Why is this happening to me?" But now, I was in *their* shoes, and the blubbering victim I was threatening was a fiendish criminal. It felt amazing!

I'm stronger than those guys. I can do whatever I want with them.

"Please, have mercy. I'll tell you everything. If—"

Goaz's pleading was really starting to piss me off. "Would you shut up already?"

To shut him up at last, I sliced Goaz's head off. Then, looking down at his body in surprise, I saw his bluish-black skin had turned a more natural tanned brown.

"His skin's back to normal. So he wasn't a cyborg?"

No machine parts protruded from the chopped stumps of his body either. *So how did he get that metallic stuff? This world is full of mysteries.*

I picked up his head and handed it to one of my men. "Will this be proof enough?"

"Y-yes!" The soldiers all rapidly saluted me.

Just then, I received a report that we'd gained full control of the ship.

"Over already, eh?"

It felt like everything had happened so quickly. There had been a ton of forces in the pirate gang, but few of them had turned out to be tough. For my first battle, it was a bit underwhelming.

One of my men brought me an additional report. "It appears there are captives on board, Lord Liam."

"Captives?"

"Yes. They were being held prisoner by the pirates."

One of the captured pirates led us toward a room near Goaz's chambers. All this time, I'd been thinking this vessel was pretty solidly built for a pirate ship, but they had apparently just stolen a battleship from some nation and modified it. It was pretty cheeky of those pirates to have done something so brash, but the nation that had their ship stolen didn't come out of it looking very good either.

I kicked the pirate who was guiding us, and he flew forward. "We're still not there yet?"

"N-no, sir!" The other pirates referred to this man as the "breeder," and he had apparently been close to Goaz. He was short, with a bulging stomach and reedy limbs. The man was more than a little creepy. Apparently, his job on the ship had required specialized knowledge.

We finally arrived at the room, and one of my men opened the door to enter before me.

The breeder looked nervous. "P-please don't touch any of the devices. It's hard to get your hands on things like this, you know."

"Devices?"

Just what kind of animals was he raising on this ship that required special devices? Did they make a profit selling them? I decided to ask him something that had been on my mind.

"Hey."

"Yes?"

"You got a dog on this ship?"

The breeder's lips pulled up in a disgusting smile as he tried to sell me on his skills. "Oh, I know all about what you nobles like; I can make you any kind of dog you want. Would you like an obedient one, or do you have a preference when it comes to looks?"

I wasn't sure how to interpret his answer. All I'd asked him was if there was a dog on board. *Is this guy okay?*

As I was thinking this, the men who'd entered the room stormed back out of it and opened the visors on their helmets, vomiting. Seeing their pitiful display, one of the men guarding me shouted, "Is that any way to act in front of Lord Liam, you lot?"

Seeing how these trained soldiers had turned blue, I became extra curious about what exactly was inside that room.

Another man exited it and reported, "I would recommend you stay out here, Lord Liam." His voice was shaky, and he hadn't even told me what he'd found, so this hardly counted as a report.

"I need to know: what's in there?"

While my men hesitated to speak, the creepy breeder spoke up instead. "This is also my laboratory, you see. I spent most of my time fulfilling the late captain's requests. I'm sure you'll like my work as well, my lord."

The soldiers who'd come out of the room glared at the man. "You pig!"

He just smirked in response. "Oh? Not to your tastes, then?"

I didn't like this guy's attitude. "Explain."

When I demanded an explanation, the breeder all too eagerly commenced describing his work.

Sickened, I borrowed a gun from one of my men and shot him through the head.

There's no value in any *of these people.*

Ominous tools lined the walls of the dark room. I spotted various strange devices and an operating table.

The pirates had called this the "stable." It was a disgusting display of the experiments done by the man called the breeder, and the abominable acts Goaz had asked him to perform—things a normal person couldn't have hoped to understand.

The *things* on display in this room were all men and women—or rather, what had once been men and women. Apparently, Goaz had enjoyed seeing beautiful people gradually made ugly, and the breeder had enjoyed modifying the human body. This combination meant the room was now full of tragic sights that had once been healthy men and women, whom Goaz had captured from planets he'd plundered and locked into these upright cylinders.

One of the women in this torture chamber had received particularly poor treatment. Her name was Christiana Leta Rosebreia—and she had once been a gorgeous female knight. Hailing from a small planet in the Intergalactic Empire, she had been born into royalty and beloved by her people. They had affectionately called her Tia and revered her strength and beauty as the Princess Knight. When Goaz had taken her entire planet hostage, she had surrendered to him, and she had survived all this time as his favorite plaything.

Others amongst the captives brought to this room had been in similar positions, and their appearances had been altered by Goaz's twisted lust.

Christiana—Tia—resided in the room as a lump of flesh, all traces of her former appearance gone. She spent her days grieving her now-destroyed homeland and wishing for the day to come when she would finally die. She had once been a noble-minded individual, but now Tia's heart was beyond the point of breaking.

Sensing the change occurring inside the ship, her suspicions were confirmed when an unfamiliar combat unit entered the room. The troops wore different equipment from the pirates and followed organized commands and therefore had to be soldiers belonging to some nation. When these soldiers entered the room and saw the tormented creatures inside, they couldn't help but retch.

Tia addressed one shaking soldier. "What happened to Goaz?"

She had once possessed a beautiful voice, but there was no trace of beauty now. This distorted voice coming from the ugly creature she had become only served to further terrify the soldier. He pointed his gun at her in fright. "Ahh!"

Seeing his reaction, Tia was reminded of just what a monstrosity she had become. The thought saddened her all over again, but at the same time, she was relieved that she would finally be freed.

"Please do not be afraid. Despite my shocking appearance, I am not your enemy. Let me ask again: what happened to Goaz?"

Yet the soldier was so afraid, he couldn't answer. In fact, he looked as though he were about to pull the trigger at any moment. However, this only brought relief to Tia and the others like her who had been transformed. *Ah, we can finally die*, they thought. For closure, they wanted to know what had become of Goaz and the breeder in the end, but Tia could barely bring herself to care anymore. She just wanted it all to end.

At that point, she heard a single gunshot from outside the room. What had happened? While she wondered this, the soldiers all lined up, and a single knight entered the room. He was small, still young, and holding a sword. She couldn't tell if he'd come of age yet. Despite this, Tia sensed from the soldiers' attitude toward him that he must have held a fairly high position.

"Was Goaz captured?" she asked him.

The boy seemed surprised that she could even speak, but he quickly answered her. "I killed him." He seemed possessed of a composure beyond his years. "I shot the breeder too."

At the boy's blunt words, Tia felt happiness for the first time since she'd been imprisoned here. "Is that so?"

The creatures in the other cylinders in the room began to emit sounds of joy, gratitude, and tearful happiness. They were overwhelmed that their tormentors were finally both dead.

While the soldiers were frightened, the boy faced Tia. One of the men who had been searching the room brought the boy a tablet.

Tia was grateful from the bottom of her heart. To her, this boy was like a messenger from the god she'd prayed to every day, sent here to free her from her hellish suffering.

"It's finally over. I do not know who you are, but if you have any compassion, please...save us." The salvation Tia begged for was death at the hands of the boy and his men. In her current body, she was not capable of granting this wish herself, but through these others her living nightmare would finally be over.

"Save you?"

"Yes. I'm sure you can understand what I mean when you see how we are now. We can never live as humans again. So please, by your hands..."

They'd been turned into disgusting travesties and could never return to their former selves. There was no point in them staying alive a minute longer.

But the boy's response was not what they expected. "Very well, I'll save you... And I expect you to return the favor. Somebody, get a medic and transport these people."

He seemed to have misunderstood her. "W-wait—"

But he took his team of soldiers and left the room. She pleaded to the remaining soldiers instead, "Please! Kill me! Just kill me!"

The soldiers averted their eyes. "We can't disobey Lord Liam's orders. Sorry."

Despair came crashing back down on Tia and the others. They had thought they were finally going to be freed, but their expectations had been cruelly betrayed.

"Please! Kill us! There's no meaning in living like this anymore!"

The cries and screams continued to echo through the chamber long after Liam had left it.

After leaving the sickening collection, I scrolled away on a tablet, learning about the original forms of the unfortunate creatures inside those tubes. There were also records of exactly what kinds of experiments had been carried out to make those beautiful men and women so grotesque, though I had no idea what was so amusing about such a pursuit. The breeder had even kept a sort of journal of each change his subjects had undergone. *I just can't understand these sadistic pirates.*

"Lord Liam, are you really going to save them?" one

of my men asked me. He seemed to have some medical knowledge. "From what I can tell, the only way to help them would be to create completely new bodies for them."

"But it can be done?"

"Y-yes. You would need magical elixirs, though. I'm sure you could dilute them, but you know what those cost, don't you?"

Elixirs in fantasy worlds are like a miracle cure-all. This world has them too, of course, but they're a rare find even in the vast Empire. When they can be found on the market, they go for ridiculous prices. Frankly, they're so expensive that a lower-class noble can't even afford them.

"Well, I've just gotta buy 'em, right? I wanted some on hand for myself anyway."

If I sell the treasure I'm nabbing from Goaz, I should earn a decent amount. Actually, Goaz might have some elixirs hidden on his ship. I'm the type who'd use my elixirs right when I get them.

"Well, er...you'd need a specialized doctor too. The facilities for their treatment would also be expensive. Considering the state they're in, they'd need psychological care as well. It would take *years* to get them back to their original bodies. I, well...I just think it'd take an unreasonable amount of money to treat them."

Well, I think I'll make plenty of money off our victory, so it shouldn't be a problem. "They asked me to save them, so I'm saving them. That's all there is to it."

"I think what they meant by that was—"

"I know."

The soldier went quiet.

I understood that they didn't have any hope of a normal life anymore. Looking over the entries in the tablet, however, I'd been struck by the unfairness of it all. I felt like I was looking at my old self—though they had gone through even more than I had—and I couldn't help but sympathize. Nearly all the people in that room had had their planet destroyed by Goaz. They didn't have a home to return to.

"I'm in a good mood right now. It doesn't hurt to do a good deed every once in a while, don't you think?"

My men didn't seem able to respond to that. Maybe they were ridiculing me on the inside for being a villain who talked about good deeds. Maybe they were holding back laughter.

Well, anyway, I've once again come out of this with a nice return on my investments. And as always, it's all thanks to the Guide.

Back in House Banfield's domain, the media reported Lord Liam's grand victory over the Goaz Pirate Gang. The whole planet rejoiced when they heard the news.

The bartender served his patrons drink after drink in celebration.

His regular at the counter proposed a toast to the bartender. "You're doing great business today, aren't you?"

The bartender drained his own drink after the toast. "I thought we were goners for sure this time." He'd felt like he was doomed the moment he heard the Goaz Pirate Gang was on the way. There had been no detailed information from the government, but as far as the average citizen understood, it wasn't a rare event for a planet to be wiped out by pirates. That was just how malignant pirates were.

The regular happily downed his drink as well. "You said it! I panicked and opened up a bottle I'd been saving for a special occasion."

The bartender laughed at this. "Bah, you should have held off! It would've only gotten better with age! Instead of drinking while fearing your death, you could have drunk it while praying for victory."

"Yeah," the regular agreed. "It was a bit of a waste. Is the rumor true that this was the count's first battle?"

"That's what the news says."

Empire nobles sometimes participated in battles out of a desire for notable achievements, but even then, they participated from the safety of the rear. However, the news was reporting that Lord Banfield had entered a mobile knight and charged the enemy flagship himself. In fact, reports went so far as to say that he had boarded the pirate ship and killed Goaz personally, but this was probably not true.

"He's like a hero from a fairy tale. If it's true, that is."

"You're right about that," the bartender agreed. He couldn't help smiling. "I prefer to believe it's true. If something were to happen to that man, I don't think I'd get to see this anymore."

The bartender and the regular both looked out at the crowd of patrons making merry in the bar. Before Liam had been born, the bartender could never have imagined a sight like this.

His regular was just as happy. "Yeah. Well, whatever the future holds, let's just celebrate our lord making it through his first battle."

The two hoisted some more drinks and toasted again.

When I returned home, I received a warm welcome. My subjects were overjoyed, and Brian was sobbing—so much that it kinda creeped me out.

"Master Liam! I knew you would return safely!"

"Oh, uh, yeah?"

"It's true that he was worried about you," Amagi whispered into my ear, "but he didn't think you would win."

"Is that so?" I shot a suspicious look at Brian, who averted his eyes.

Well, I guess I should be happy that he was so worried about me.

"Anyway, how were things back here? No problems, I hope?"

Brian gave me all sorts of information, but I couldn't really make any of it out through his sobbing. In the end, I had to ask Amagi for clarification.

"I got a summons from the Capital Planet?"

"Yes. You are to be rewarded with a medal for your triumph over the Goaz Pirate Gang. A more official summons should be coming soon."

The Guide had said something about that, hadn't he? Fame and prestige and what have you.

I've obtained treasure and prestige just from taking out some lame pirate gang. Pirate-hunting might not be a bad hobby.

"There were messages from the Henfrey Company and the Seventh Weapons Factory as well. Master Thomas wished to discuss purchasing your spoils of war."

"The Weapons Factory too?" That was where Nias worked, though I couldn't help but think her pretty face would be better served elsewhere. I wasn't sure what they wanted from me.

"Many of the pirates' weapons were made in other nations," Amagi explained. "The factory would like to purchase them for research."

"Guess they're passionate about their work."

"They may have also heard that we discovered some rare metals, so they may want to acquire them as production materials."

The Goaz Pirate Gang had been in possession of a large quantity of precious metals. They didn't have a ton of gold, though, so I wasn't very excited about the rest.

"Meeting with Thomas comes first."

"I shall arrange it immediately."

It's definitely nice to have competent people working for you.

I'M THE **EVIL LORD** OF AN **INTERGALACTIC EMPIRE**

13 Family

A MONTH AFTER THE BATTLE, things had pretty much settled down. Well, my staff was still busy taking care of various related affairs afterward, but things had settled down for *me*. Anyway, it was appropriate that they should be busy and I should be idle. I was the ruler, after all.

Anyway, I sat in my meeting room across from Echigoya—I mean Thomas.

"Thomas, you're quite wicked yourself!"

"Huh?! No, I would say these are quite reasonable prices."

I'd entrusted Thomas Henfrey with buying up the precious metals, curios, and other valuables we'd acquired from the pirates, but the price he quoted me was so ridiculous that I had to laugh. It had so many digits, I wasn't quite able to wrap my head around it. That was just how vast the treasure accumulated by the Goaz Pirate Gang was.

"Just adhering to the script," I assured him.

"I-is that so?" he said, still not accustomed to my skit. "Are you really all right with letting go of it all, though?"

I was selling off almost all the precious metals and treasures I'd acquired. Why? Well, to pay off my debt, of course. I'd be able to make a huge dent in it this way, though it wouldn't wipe out the whole thing. Just how much money had this noble family burned through, anyway? It boggled the mind that my debt exceeded the value of the treasures Goaz had amassed for himself.

"What good would it do me to keep any more of this stuff? I've held on to a few items, you know—like this sword."

I showed him the blade I'd taken a liking to, and Thomas looked quite impressed.

"You've got your hands on something amazing."

"Oh? Have I?" I'd just been thinking of it as a sword with an excellent blade, but apparently it was worth more than that.

"I'm not an expert or anything, but even I can tell that it's something special. Would you like to have it appraised by a specialist?"

"Hmm... Nah, not really. I plan on using it as my personal weapon anyway."

"Huh?" Thomas looked up at me as if he wanted to ask, "You're going to *use* a sword like this?" As I was in a good mood today, I just smiled at him.

"Hey, I took a liking to it."

"I-is that so?" Thomas still seemed surprised, but the weapon was highly functional, so I was intent on continuing to make use of it.

He went on, "Now, about the goods you've requested. I'll have them sent here as soon as possible."

I had ordered medical equipment through Thomas. I figured this was a good opportunity to get my hands on some of the stuff I'd be needing. I had plenty of new patients who required unique treatment, after all.

"I'm counting on you to find those medical specialists too."

"Leave it to me, my lord."

It really is handy having a personal merchant. I mean, he can even find personnel for me. The guy's probably milking me to make a fortune himself, though. That pisses me off a little.

"When will you be heading for the Capital Planet, Lord Liam?"

"Next year. I'll go before my coming-of-age ceremony. I'm gonna be busy for a while after that."

In this world, people reached adulthood at age fifty, and when a noble became an adult, his life became a lot more complicated. I would have to start taking classes in order to become a "proper noble," and I wasn't looking forward to it. I wanted to start on that whole "evil lord" thing, but I wouldn't even be able to go back to my own domain for a while after I received that award on the Capital Planet.

"I will make sure to be present at your conferment ceremony. Oh, and here are the yellow sweets you always request."

"Echigoya, you're quite wicked yourself!"

"As I continue to remind you, it is the Henfrey Company, my lord."

I love how you never forget your bribe—my gratuity, that is.

The Seventh Weapons Factory was built on a moon in space. It was common to mine these natural satellites for their resources and establish facilities like this on the surface. These outposts primarily manufactured weapons but did other types of work as well, such as studying and testing weapons acquired from other interstellar empires.

Nias, who had been promoted to an engineering captain, felt deeply moved as she stood before the rows upon rows of pirate ships sent by House Banfield.

"It's incredible. I wasn't expecting much from pirate ships, but they're all *battleships*. The modifications to the armor are in pretty poor taste, though."

One of her subordinates, standing beside her to look out at all the warships, couldn't understand it either. "Why do they make them so flashy? Ah well. This is just an incredible haul. Not to mention all the loose material we can work with too."

Nias sighed. "I was a little hasty in buying them, so I'm scared to see next year's budget. I don't suppose we could arrange another big sales order, could we?"

She was thinking about how to get Liam to purchase another fleet from them.

"You gonna seduce him again?" Her subordinate laughed.

"Hey, stop. Why are you laughing?"

"Sorry. But yeah, we really could use a regular customer, couldn't we?"

The Seventh Weapons Factory's budget was in a precarious state after losing out in so many of the Imperial Army's preliminary trials. Still, they hadn't just bought up the vessels and materials from Liam on a whim.

"We're not gonna lose out next time. We can make back all our investments if we use these assets to develop a next-generation ship."

"That's not gonna be easy."

"I know that!"

Nias turned on her heel and stormed off to work, grumpy with her subordinate's pessimism.

The Empire's central planet and the seat of its government was known as the Capital Planet. The year after my battle with Goaz, I headed there for a ceremony where I would receive a medal.

I had heard that the Capital Planet was something else, and once I arrived, I had to agree. *I mean, to surround an entire planet...*

Imagine a sphere of metal large enough to envelop an entire planet, which was just what the Empire had done. Its Capital Planet was fully encapsulated by liquid metal. This metal made it possible to regulate and manipulate the planet's weather, and it doubled as a powerful defensive wall. The first time I saw it, I thought, *Was the guy who thought this up an idiot or a genius?*

From the spaceport, I descended to the planet via

space elevator, arriving in a concrete jungle. Well, it wasn't concrete per se, but gargantuan gray buildings surrounded me in such a cluster that it was as though the planet were made up of machines. There just wasn't enough green.

This was a world of towering skyscrapers, with a population in the tens of billions. When I heard that, it was so awe-inspiring, I wasn't really able to think anything other than *Wow, the Empire's something else.* Of course, if you were to ask if I was jealous, I wouldn't be sure how to answer. It was so overwhelming, I couldn't really find it in me to envy it.

On the day of the ceremony, while I waited in a room of the palace, two couples came to see me. Each looked like nothing more than a married couple in their twenties.

I'd been checking over my attire in the waiting room, but now I was forced to puzzle over the appearance of these four strangers. One of them had greeted me very familiarly, after all.

"Long time no see, Liam."

"Huh? Who're you?"

The atmosphere in the waiting room grew exceedingly awkward, the smile of the man who'd spoken becoming strained. "W-well, it's been a while—I guess you don't recognize me. Have I gotten that much older?"

"I have no idea who you are." I thought for sure these people would turn out to be some self-proclaimed "relatives" who'd come to extort me for money now that I had achieved notoriety. I'd heard once in my previous life that when you became famous, you tended to suddenly gain family members you'd never known before. Of course, in *my* life it was the opposite; all my relatives had abandoned me. If you're doing poorly, they leave; if you're doing well, they gather. That was what I figured was going on here.

I did experience a vague sense of familiarity, but it was probably just my imagination. By now, all four of them looked rather uncomfortable, so I turned to Amagi for clarification.

"Who are they, Amagi?" I'd thought about leaving her behind to oversee my domain, but this was a big moment for me, and I wanted her by my side for it. Brian was watching over the mansion. He cried over every little thing, so I'd been too embarrassed to bring him.

"Master, these two are your parents. The two behind them would be your grandparents."

Parents? Oh yeah... I did have those, didn't I? Two poor fools whose social status and territory were stolen by—no, wait. They foisted their debt onto me. Now I'm mad.

My old man, Cliff, cleared his throat in an overly deliberate way. "It appears you remember us now. I suppose if you haven't seen someone in over forty years, you could forget their face. As your father, though, I'm a little shocked."

Uhh, I don't remember you ever doing anything particularly fatherly for me.

Darcie, my old lady, tried to laugh it off. "You're such a kidder, Liam. I see you're still taking good care of the doll I bought you. I don't know if you should be bringing it to the palace, though."

"What?" This ticked me off, but the couple who claimed to be my grandparents made it even worse.

"I must say, it's a bit disappointing to be meeting my grandson for the first time, only to find that he's brought a doll to the palace. You're almost an adult, boy. It's time to throw that thing away."

My grandmother said, "My husband's right—it's pathetic. And here you're supposed to be the head of House Banfield."

The two of them looked like they couldn't have been older than thirty, so this all seemed like some sort of joke. Still, it wasn't unusual in this world, where anti-aging technology was very advanced and people could look young at any given age.

Amagi bowed her head and made to leave. "I shall wait in another room."

I stopped her. "There's no need—you'll be staying with me. Anyway, what do you want?" I asked, feeling agitated.

The four of them took turns in replying. "We heard you'd be receiving a tremendous reward, and we'd like you to share some of it with us. Our debts have increased, and we're in a bit of trouble."

"It's expensive living in the capital, so if you have some extra funds, it would be nice if you'd increase our allowance."

Increase their allowance because the capital's costly? Who is the kid and who are the parents here? Our positions are reversed!

"I've already placed some orders with a merchant, so I trust you're good for the money."

"It makes me so proud to have such an accomplished grandson."

It made me furious to think that these were the people who had ruined my planet. This was *my* money, *my* domain. *I'm not giving you anything!*

"Amagi, see our visitors out."

When I tried to dismiss them, Cliff started to panic. I must have totally surprised him.

"Liam, how could you do this to your parents?!"

"I don't owe you anything."

The only parents I have are my mother and father from my previous life. Who the hell cares about you guys? Sorry, but you're not gonna get any warm, fuzzy feelings from me. Get used to it; I'm a villain.

I kicked my parents and grandparents out of the room, even though the palace maids were watching. As an awkward air permeated the room, I addressed Amagi. "Do I really have to pay back their debts?"

"If you do not, I imagine the creditors and merchants will come to you to collect."

"What a nuisance." I looked around me, and it felt like all the people in our vicinity were holding their breaths.

Amagi made a suggestion. "Perhaps you should adjust their allowance. You could increase the amount on the condition that they keep their distance from now on. I believe that is your best option. Raising a fuss will only harm your reputation, Master."

Honestly, I wanted to just get rid of them, but that seemed like a whole different kind of trouble.

"Prepare the paperwork. I'll spare them some pocket change at least."

"Certainly."

A ways away from the ceremony space, a lone figure walked with his hand trailing against the wall, looking rather exhausted. It was the Guide.

"Damn you... Damn you, Liam..." he muttered in resentment.

He had used too much of his energy on Goaz, so now he was unable to flee to another world. As Liam's thankfulness grew, the Guide underwent daily torture. To make matters worse, Liam's defeat of Goaz had further boosted the support of his subjects and only increased his power. This boy had become the bane of the Guide's existence, now that he carried with him the gratitude of his citizens on top of his own.

"How did he defeat Goaz? He shouldn't have been able to wound him. How the hell did he find *that* sword at that exact moment?"

Liam *should* have lost. The Guide had let his guard down and used up too much of his power, and now Liam's appreciation was eating away at him, sapping his strength.

"He won't get away with this. I won't let him." He ground his teeth, heading for the room where Liam's parents and grandparents had gone following their audience with him. No one walking through the halls of the palace noticed the Guide. When he stepped into the room, he found the four people inside arguing in front of a digital document.

"This is all your fault for not educating him properly!"

"Oh, that's rich coming from you! What did *you* do for me?!"

Liam had had Amagi draw up a contract that stated he would increase the amount of money they were regularly sent, as long as they agreed to never interact with him again. Unsatisfied, Liam's relatives debated how to squeeze more money out of him now that he was so successful.

Clearly, they were complete scum, but exactly the sort of scum that the Guide loved using and later ruining. Right now, however, he had no room to consider bringing them additional misfortune. Standing nearby, the Guide smiled bravely through his pain and spoke to them, though they didn't consciously hear him.

"I'm afraid you four are going to have to do some work for me. It's tradition for royals to engage in endless power struggles. Liam, your family is going to take everything from you. They shall be your worst enemy."

The Guide was so weakened, he didn't even have the strength to check in on Liam anymore. His options had become severely limited. Despite this, he managed to work up a black smoke, which burst from his body and enveloped the four.

Liam's grandfather's eyes suddenly widened, as if he'd just remembered something. "I know—let's apply for an official change of family headship. If we do that, we can take control of all of Liam's assets."

His grandmother clapped her hands together in agreement. "That's a great idea. I'll ask a friend of mine in the palace to fast-track the paperwork."

Cliff began conspiring with Darcie about what they could do to contribute. "Let's create another heir, then. Liam just didn't work out."

Darcie's expression made it clear she didn't see any other way. "I suppose you're right. If it means coming into a territory with great wealth, then I can do that much. What will you do with Liam, though?"

With grim determination, Cliff decided to make use of a shady tactic. "If we can obtain enough money, we'll be able to hire as many assassins as we want. It would be suspicious right after the ceremony, though. We'll just have Liam disappear sometime after the succession."

Having heard these plans, the Guide was satisfied. "Looks like this time it's goodbye for real, Liam."

He vanished from the room, and a small light hovering in the corner exited straight through the closed door.

Amagi had been aware that she would not be able to attend the proceedings herself, so when Liam went to participate in the ceremony, she headed to another room to await his return. The Empire was not a kind place for dolls.

Liam had wanted her to be present during the entire ceremony, but Amagi had strongly refused for fear of damaging his reputation. She planned to watch the event from a screen in the waiting room. However, on her way there, she came upon a strange sight.

"What is that?"

She had discovered a light floating in front of a door. This light then slipped right through the closed door, leaving Amagi standing in front of it. Curious, she scanned the situation inside the room, finding four signs of life inside. She determined they belonged to Liam's parents and grandparents. When she touched the door, she intercepted the conversation they were having inside.

"What'll we say to justify the reason for wanting to switch headship?"

"Whatever. We can say he's unfit to be an Imperial noble since he keeps a doll by his side. There's that. Plus, we could bribe someone in the palace to come up with some other reason for us."

"And the assassins?"

"I have someone I can contact about that..."

After eavesdropping, Amagi swiftly left the area. *I'll have to part with Master soon*, she thought to herself.

If she stayed by his side, Liam would lose his standing, and Amagi certainly didn't want that.

The ceremony was held outside. Blue skies and warm sunlight, not too bright, had been set for the occasion. I couldn't believe that all of this was artificial.

Amid this heavenly, orchestrated setting, I knelt in front of His Imperial Majesty. He was so far away that I couldn't hear his actual voice, instead listening to the enormous 3D image of him projected in the sky above me. There was a long preamble, followed by some other talk, including responses required from me, and then I received my medal.

All around me were nobles gathered to attend the ceremony. And what a number of them! *There really are a ton of these guys.*

This austere ceremony continued for some time, I received some more appreciative words in closing, and then it was finally over. At no point did I have an opportunity to talk directly with the emperor.

That's just the way of things, I suppose.

After the ceremony ended, I decided to stay on the Capital Planet to experience it for a while, and what awaited me there was…party invitations. They came almost daily. Apparently, there was always some great festival or big celebration happening somewhere or other. Since I figured it fitted the stereotype of an evil noble to be seen at such parties, I made sure to attend. It wasn't like there was an entry fee, and it felt nice to be fawned over.

Therefore, my days in the capital were fairly busy, and Amagi seemed preoccupied with a task of her own. Whenever I asked her what it was, she would always just say, "It is fine. I took care of it."

Well, if she was taking care of things, I figured it was fine for me to continue attending parties, so tonight I was preparing for yet another one.

"How's it look?" I'd put on some new clothes and modeled them for Amagi. Once you'd worn a certain outfit to a party, you could never wear the same one again. It was a complete waste, if you asked me.

"It suits you wonderfully, Master."

Despite Amagi's compliment, something felt off about her.

"Amagi, are you hiding something from me?"

"I would never. You will be late to your party, so you should depart now."

She rushed me out the door, and I headed on my way.

14 Gratitude

THE IMPERIAL PALACE was so large that it was practically a metropolis; it was hard to tell exactly where it began and ended. One particularly large building on the palace grounds was the workplace of the prime minister, and every individual within this looming skyscraper was under the prime minister's employ.

In an office on the building's top floor, a gray-haired old man was trying to deal with the work before him while also hearing out a younger man who had requested an audience. The younger of the two was Cliff, Liam's father.

"What is the meaning of this, Your Excellency? Why will you not approve our change of headship?!"

The fact that most nobles appeared to be in their twenties was proof of just how many years the prime minister had been alive. He had served several generations of emperors and was said to know everything there was to know about the Empire.

"Some years ago, you applied for succession. It was approved, so there is no reason to overturn that decision now."

Whereas the prime minister was dispassionate, Cliff was incensed. "The boy brought a doll to the Imperial Palace. He is simply too unaware of what it means to be an Imperial noble. Would you have House Banfield simply bear this humiliation?"

The prime minister sighed and finally looked up from the documents on his tablet. "Is Lord Liam not a fine noble? He runs his territory so effectively and even eliminated a fleet of space pirates. The Empire does not punish nobles for keeping dolls—it is simply not customary."

"And there is a reason for that custom, is there not?! Please rethink this, Your Excellency!"

The old man offered a crinkled smile. Cliff took that to mean his passion was finally getting through to the man, but soon enough, his own face paled.

"Lord Liam is fulfilling his obligations and paying his taxes, unlike the lords who came before him. He is a splendid noble who is contributing to the betterment of the Empire, and we have high hopes for him. Do you understand my meaning?"

"Erm, well... In that case, I swear to you that we will pay our dues upon your approval, so there should be no problems."

Looking well and truly amused, the prime minister laughed. "You want us to trust you to do something you've never done before? You lot and that boy are possessed of vastly different characters. The reason you're able to petition me this shamelessly is that you can't even understand which of you would be more beneficial to the Empire."

Cliff's mouth opened and closed as he tried to come up with an argument, but the other man didn't give him a chance to speak.

"I wouldn't do anything rash if I were you. If you want to keep living quietly in the capital, that is."

To Cliff, there was a message between the lines: "If you do anything to Liam, we'll erase you." Defeated, he left the office on unsteady feet.

The prime minister watched him leave, appalled. "The standards of nobility really have dropped in recent times. I still can't believe *that* man produced a son of such caliber."

Not only had the boy revived a waning domain, he'd defeated a fleet of pirates in an outnumbered battle. Actually, an outstanding lord in a remote region who excelled in both political and military matters was a bit of a worry for the prime minister. Such an individual might turn against the Empire one day, after all. The Empire would never lose, of course, but it would make for trouble. If Liam remained loyal, then that was different. The prime minister was very fond of nobles who dutifully paid their taxes and followed directives.

"Why would I want to grant headship to someone who's no use to the Empire? I'd rather that boy Liam continue to work faithfully for us."

He checked over a particular digital document. It detailed Liam's reward for vanquishing the pirate gang.

Liam had declined the reward. More specifically, he had put it toward the arrears on his taxes. At the same time, he'd used his other profits from the battle to order a dreadnought from an Empire-controlled factory, and he was requesting authorization for the purchase.

Neither of those actions harmed the Empire; in fact, it would profit from them. Not only would they not have to pay Liam his reward, but he was even making a purchase from an Imperial factory. The prime minister was constantly finding some new reason to stress over the Empire's finances, so he was thrilled with both proposals. In Liam's case, he wasn't obtaining a reward for all his hard work, and all he was really getting was permission to own a flagship.

Scanning another document, he murmured, "A doll who protects her master, hmm?"

This one was a report from Amagi on the actions of Liam's relatives. Amagi had met in secret with the prime minister, arranging for him to decline Cliff's proposal to change the headship in exchange for Liam not accepting his reward.

"She is utterly devoted to the boy, while his own blood relatives are trying to drive him out for their selfish desires. It truly is a sad world we live in."

The prime minister shook his head, taking a short break before he resumed his work.

In an expensive suite in a high-class capital hotel, I rested on my bed with my head in Amagi's lap.

"I just don't get it, Amagi. What *are* parties?"

After participating in them day and night for some time now, I had begun to seriously consider just what these parties were for. They were all so elaborate and unique. I had eaten creatures I'd never even heard of and marveled at entertainment I'd never before experienced. The one that had surpassed my imagination the most was the bucket party. Hearing the name "bucket party," I was tempted to make fun of it even before I attended. Honestly, I wondered how people even came up with ideas like that. Well, it certainly left me with an appreciation for the infinite possibilities of buckets.

Other worlds sure are something else.

"I had no idea what you could do with buckets. I still can't believe it."

Amagi stroked my head gently. "Did you not enjoy yourself?"

"Quite the opposite. I was just so surprised." My heart was still tickled by the lingering excitement.

I was also enjoying the blissful feeling of Amagi's lap—until she rained on my parade.

"You are almost an adult now, Master. I have served you for over forty years."

"Feels like a long time, but somehow short too."

This timespan had been longer than my entire previous life, yet it had gone by in a flash.

"You should no longer keep me at your side."

I sat up. "What's this all about?"

Amagi explained matter-of-factly, "The Empire has a negative view of dolls. Your reputation will suffer while I stand beside you, Master. I would suggest making a human woman your companion instead."

Amagi's comments were a bolt from the blue. "I-is this some sort of joke?"

"It is not."

"Huh?" I was suddenly reminded of my wife from my last life.

"It will be better for you this way."

I remembered the woman who had told me she loved me and then all too easily abandoned me. The woman who had gotten together with another man and spurned me. The woman I'd hated so much once I discovered the truth that I'd wanted to kill her.

"I see—you're abandoning me. Just be honest and tell me you don't want to be with me anymore!" I stood up, shouting, "Even a *doll* will abandon me?!"

"No," Amagi said with a shake of her head. "I have thoroughly enjoyed the time I have spent with you, Master. That is exactly why we must part. In addition, I am now an outdated model. A more efficient—"

So what? That's *why you want to leave me?*

"Don't be ridiculous! All you need to do is follow my orders! So, it's an order, then: stay by my side forever. You can't disobey my orders—isn't that right, Amagi?"

Amagi hung her head. "If that is your order, I shall obey."

That's right. You should've just done that from the beginning.

"You should've just said that. You can't... You can't abandon me too." I started to cry, and Amagi stroked my head.

"Whatever am I to do with you, Master?"

Now that I think about it, she's been with me for almost a half a century. She's more important to me now than my wife from my past life.

"Hasn't it always been the two of us?" I said, tears flowing down my cheeks.

After a short pause, she replied, "Mister Brian has always been with you too, has he not? He has been your companion since you were born, in fact, so Mister Brian has been with you longer."

What? I mean, yeah, but Brian doesn't count; he's in a different category.

"Don't bring Brian into this. That's not what I meant."

Amagi smiled when I said that. The expression looked truly heartfelt, not one you would think a doll was capable of. Still, there was something sad about it.

"I shall endeavor to serve at your side for as long as I am able, then."

"Good. As you should."

Jeez. Don't scare me like that. I was relieved, but also strangely nervous. What was that touch of sadness I thought I'd seen in Amagi's smile just now?

When she awakened, she felt very strange. The sensations of her body felt nostalgic somehow, and the ceiling above her wasn't the ceiling she was used to seeing, of that horrible breeder's room.

"Where am I?" she muttered. Turning her head, she saw what looked like a hospital room around her. Her body was moving in ways she wasn't used to. It felt like she had her old arms and legs back, almost as if she were in a dream.

After a little while, she heard a door open, and a male doctor in a white lab coat entered. For a moment, she tensed up, but it wasn't the breeder.

"I see you're awake." There was no disgust in the doctor's eyes as he looked down at Tia.

"Pardon, but where am I?" Her voice sounded different. It was as though her old, lost voice had returned, but perhaps younger than she recalled.

A nurse came from behind the doctor to check on Tia. Now that her head was clearing, she noticed that the ceiling was a mirror; she could see herself in it. At first she looked away, not wanting to see herself, but the Tia in the mirror was her former self. She looked just as she had shortly after becoming an adult.

Long, flaxen, glossy hair. Pale skin and vibrant pink lips. Green eyes. Yes: it was her old face, which she hadn't seen in so long.

"Huh? What's going...?" As she stared at herself in confusion, tears began spilling from her eyes. She was *human*.

But she couldn't move her face very well, or her arms and legs. Her whole body wasn't responding as she wanted it to.

The doctor gave her a reassuring look. "We completely regenerated your body from scratch. It took quite a long time."

Tia couldn't believe what he was telling her. "You brought my body back?"

The doctor looked awkward as he tried to summarize the situation. "It took an elixir to do it, though. Your body is now the same as it was before, but you'll need intense rehabilitation to move like you used to."

As former royalty, Tia was well aware of the value of such a miracle drug.

"Elixir? You used something so valuable for me?"

"Well, it was diluted. Anyway, like I said, the rehabilitation will be harsh. After all, we basically rebuilt your entire body."

Is this a dream? Tia wondered. She didn't care if it was; she was just happy it was a good one.

"I'll do it. I'll do anything! This really is just like a dream," Tia said, and the doctor smiled.

"It's no dream. This is real."

At the doctor's words, fresh tears spilled from Tia's eyes. There was one thing she was curious about, though. From what she understood about full-body regeneration, it wasn't something that just anyone could receive. Unlike regenerating one lost or damaged body part, in order to regenerate someone completely, you would need a specialized facility and a brilliant medical specialist as well. This was the sort of thing that *could* be done, but typically wasn't. After all, the only people who could make use of elixirs were nobles and the extremely wealthy. It was true that Tia had once been royalty, but her nation had been destroyed. At this point, her life didn't seem worth an elixir, so it was only natural that she wondered if she had been saved due to a misunderstanding.

"Umm, may I ask who it was who requested my treatment? If there's been a mistake, I promise I'll pay back the medical expenses after my rehabilitation. Please just give me some time."

The doctor tapped away at a tablet while explaining Tia's circumstances. "Please, don't worry—there's been no mistake, and you don't need to pay anything. Lord Banfield has covered all your medical expenses. Actually, the count built this hospital and hired the staff for it specifically to treat all of the people held captive by the pirates."

"A-all of them?!"

He hadn't just sent them off somewhere with the proper facilities, but he had built an entire hospital himself. Tia could hardly believe it. Never mind the fact that he'd rescued all of them in the first place. If she had been in the count's place, she might have given up on them. The choice he'd made was just that extraordinary.

Count Banfield, huh? I wonder just what sort of person he is. He must be someone truly remarkable.

"The count's message for you is this: 'I expect you to return the favor.' Whatever that entails. For now, please just concentrate on recovering. We'll need to make sure you're mentally recovered as well as physically, after all."

When the doctor passed on the count's message, it dawned on Tia that a boy had said those same words to her just recently.

"Was he...that knight on the ship?"

"Well, if you're already familiar with the message, then I think you know the answer."

The doctor then began to describe the plans for her treatment.

I finally returned to House Banfield's domain from the Capital Planet.

Before I knew it, I'd spent a whole year in the capital. Well, things were pretty interesting there. I basically spent every day just fooling around, but if you live like that for a year, you're bound to get tired of it at some point. Since I'd grown weary of partying, I used checking up on my domain as my excuse to head back.

Upon arriving home, I received all sorts of reports from Brian in my office.

Smiling, he told me, "Master Liam, someone from the hospital contacted us to say the treatment is going well."

"What hospital?" At first, I wasn't sure what he was talking about.

Brian's smile stiffened. "You forgot? Remember the prisoners you saved from the Goaz Pirate Gang?"

"Oh, them."

Come to think of it, I did build a hospital for them, didn't I? Well, I just figured my domain could use a good-sized hospital I know I can trust. I already planned on building one at some point, so it was just a matter of good timing. But those captives—of course. So their treatment's going well?

"Yes. Those still requiring treatment should be fully recovered in a few more years, and those finished with their procedures have received aid, so they can start a life here in your domain."

Most of them had lost their homelands, so this would be their new home. They were all beautiful, and some were artists or possessed of a special skill. Maybe in the future, they'd have beautiful daughters who could become part of my harem. Hopefully, helping the refugees was an investment.

"That's wonderful." It was an economic decision as an evil lord and almost made me want to sing my own praises.

"Yes. They are all grateful to you, Master Liam."

The people I'd saved felt they owed me, which made it all worth it. This discussion put me in a good mood. I then recalled something else related to the Goaz Pirate Gang incident.

I opened a drawer and pulled out a gold box, taking a closer look at it. "Come to think of it, this is one of the things I took from Goaz." I hadn't brought it with me when I went to the Capital Planet, having simply stowed it away in this drawer.

Brian gave me an exasperated look. "You do love gold, don't you, Master Liam?"

"With a capital L."

"Hrm. Something about that box seems familiar." Brian clapped his hands together. "Now I remember!"

"What? Is it some amazing treasure?"

"No, I don't think so."

"Then don't get my hopes up. So, what did you remember?" *If I didn't know you for as long as I have, I would have your head for disappointing me like that.*

"In my younger days, I was an adventurer, you see."

By "adventurer," Brian essentially meant he'd been a space explorer. They were a fearless bunch who discovered ruins, investigated ancient civilizations, that sort of thing—not that any of it interested me. I wanted treasure, but I could do without adventure.

"Brian the adventurer, eh?"

"Yes. I recall seeing data about this artifact once. I'm sure it's just a replica, but this appears to be the alchemy box, a relic of a great, ancient magical society."

"An alchemy box? Really?"

"It's a rather fantastical story, but from what I heard, it was a tool that could turn common material into gold. I believe it's said that it could transmute any inorganic matter. For instance, you could take any rock lying by the side of the road and turn it into mithril, orichalcum, or adamantite."

"So I could use it to create gold?!"

"Huh? Ah, yes."

This world has such fantastic tools! To think I could mass-produce gold. What would I do with it all? Well, I wouldn't have to worry about my debt anymore, for one thing. I wish this one were real.

Brian seemed to share my opinion. "It really would be fantastic. If you could get a hold of the real thing, the family's financial worries would be solved just like that."

"Should I go searching for the real thing, then?"

Brian looked stern. "You are the head of House Banfield, Master Liam—a count. I'm afraid you can't go off playing adventurer."

What? Is he mad at me?

That night in my room, I contemplated the golden box.

"Man, if this were the real thing..."

I'd had Brian show me the data on the item in question, which also indicated how to use it. The ancient civilization that had created it was long gone, so the means of manufacturing the alchemy box had been lost; another one could never be made. If I could just get my hands on it, I would be free from this debt for good.

"Let's see... To use it, you just had to open the lid and concentrate, huh?"

I opened the box's lid and concentrated on a wooden practice sword in my hand, just to see what would happen.

"Yeah, right."

Having figured the thing was just a replica, I was surprised when the box responded and several screens popped up around me.

"Huh?"

The passages were written in ancient script, but I was able to decipher them thanks to my time in the education capsule.

"Convert? Er... This?"

I chose which substance to convert the wooden sword to, and it was engulfed in golden particles, changing color. When the effect had passed and I lifted the weapon higher, it no longer had the lightness of a wooden sword. It carried the weight of metal—of gold.

"No way! This is the real thing?!"

Now that I thought about it, Goaz had been excessively rich for a pirate, and he'd possessed a lot of rare metals. This must have been the source of much of his wealth.

"The Guide *said* Goaz had a great treasure of some kind, didn't he? He must have meant this."

I opened the window in my room, as if to announce my joy to the world, and laughed loudly.

"This is fantastic! The Guide even had a bonus like this in store for me! Seriously, what a great guy! Now I can do whatever I want! I can be the kind of evil lord I've been waiting to be!"

I thanked the Guide from the bottom of my heart. I was practically bursting with gratitude for the guy!

"Guide, I'm sorry I thought you were kinda suspicious at first. I'm really happy, and it's all because of you. I don't even know what to say. I feel like I'll never be able to thank you enough. Still, I want to say it... Thank you so much!"

I hope these feelings reach him!

Meanwhile, in a field illuminated by moonlight...

Bombarded by Liam's passionate feelings, the Guide's heart was burning, truly scorching, as if red-hot metal were being pressed against his chest.

"STOP IIIIIIT!" he screamed.

Weeping in agony, he clutched his chest with both hands and writhed on the ground, his legs flailing wildly. He'd thrown his suitcase aside the moment the head-splitting pain had assaulted him.

"My power... All my power is fading away!"

What little power had remained in him was stolen away now, with no hope of recovery. Because of this, he couldn't even kill Liam anymore, even if he didn't have to worry about appearances. The Guide remained curled up for some time, clutching his chest and grinding his teeth.

"You won't get away with this, Liam... I won't allow it. No matter what I have to do, I'll find a way to make your life an eternity of pain and torment. And in your unending hell, you'll hate and resent me...fear and curse me...and I'll just *laugh*."

The Guide slowly got to his feet, vowing vengeance against Liam.

"I swear it! I *swear* that I will..."

Hiding nearby in the field, a dog watched over the Guide.

Epilogue

FORTY-FIVE YEARS after reincarnating, I'd finally reached adulthood in this world. I stood in front of a mirror and looked myself over, dissatisfied.

"I still look like this after fifty years, huh?"

The kid staring back at me looked no older than thirteen. I felt like I was still in middle school. I was sure I would grow more eventually, but I was still so short.

All my servants were crying, though the only one crying loudly enough to weird me out was Brian.

"It moves me to see you all grown up, Master Liam!"

"Would you stop that? Amagi, what are my plans for the day?"

Amagi spoke dispassionately as usual. "Your coming-of-age ceremony will begin in one hour. At noon, there will be a party, but it will be more of a meet-and-greet than a meal. Then tonight there will be a banquet—"

Brian stopped crying and wiped his eyes, adding, "Incidentally, your schedule is full tomorrow as well."

Since coming home from the capital a month ago, I had been busy with work.

"Cancel all of it!"

"You cannot," Brian said, his face turning grave.

I winced, and Amagi started to hurry me along.

"You will not make it if you do not leave soon, Master."

"Yeah, yeah. Don't rush me," I grumbled as I left the room and headed for the ceremony hall.

When I'd returned from the Capital Planet, I'd had a new mansion built right away. I spent way too much money on it, and it ended up being more immense than I could have envisioned. It was basically the size of a city from my former life. I'd summoned well-known architects and artists and spared no expense, but to give you an idea of how insanely vast it was, I had to use vehicles to travel through its halls.

When I left the dressing room, Christiana was waiting for me. She stood outside in her showy blue-and-white knight garb. She'd been fully restored to her true form, a peerless beauty identifiable with a single glance. Her outfit included a white cape, and at her hip, she carried a sword specialized for piercing—a rapier. I'd heard she was quite skilled with it too.

"You look wonderful, Lord Liam."

She complimented my over-the-top outfit for the ceremony. *Hey, I love flatterers. It's proof the person cares about pleasing me, after all.* I decided to tease her with a joke.

"I was just thinking I look too good for this ceremony."

"Yes! I'm sure anything would look good on you, Lord Liam!"

What is this? It almost sounds like she's being serious. Probably just my imagination.

"Oh yeah? Anyway, are you really okay with starting to work so soon?"

According to what I'd heard from the hospital, she'd undergone rehabilitation so intense, it would have made any adult cry. Not only that, but she'd finished it in just a year, then volunteered to serve me as a knight. Everyone was singing her praises.

"Yes, it's no problem. However, in order to gain the qualifications to be an Imperial knight, I'll have to leave your domain. I wish I could serve at your side right now."

Christiana—or Tia, as she was called—was from another nation, so she was unqualified to be an Imperial knight. In order to gain those qualifications, she'd have to graduate from at least two schools, undergo special training, and gain practical experience. In total, she'd be gone for thirty years.

"Well, I'm gonna be busy now that I'm an adult too. When am I even gonna be able to come back here, I wonder?"

We all boarded a shuttle, which set off as soon as we were seated. It was a strange sight, this vehicle that looked like a carriage moving through the wide hallway. *Needing a taxi to move through your own house... Yeah, this is bizarre.*

As I lounged on a luxurious couch, Tia chatted with me.

"I swear I will serve you well, Lord Liam."

"Okay, take it easy."

She seemed really pumped up, which was fine and all, but I'd only hired her for her looks. I'd heard she was a famous knight back home, but all I cared about was having a pretty woman serving me. After all, it was the privilege of an evil lord to have beautiful ladies waiting on him, at least according to my vision.

Brian, who had no idea of my true motives, was just emotional that I was finally gaining a knight.

"At last, a trusted knight for House Banfield, Master Liam. We have nothing to worry about now."

House Banfield's previous vassals had moved away, and for a long time, no one had wanted to work for us. Now that I had made a name for myself there were knights who wanted to serve me. I didn't have any interest in tending to that, so I left the hiring to Amagi and Tia. I made the occasional comment when one of them was good-looking, though.

We could finally see our destination up ahead, but it would still be a while before we reached it.

"I made this place too big."

It was too late now, but I already regretted building my mansion this huge. I basically just got carried away with showing off how rich and powerful I was, but the thing ended up being so gargantuan that it left me speechless. Clearly, I had underestimated the space age. I mean, it was appropriately impressive for someone of my station, but the mansion I'd lived in previously had been large enough. There was just some part of me that felt I had to go to extremes if I wanted to be an evil lord. Bad guys just *had* to live in big, gaudy mansions.

The road to being an evil lord is tougher than I thought.

Among the guests in the ceremony hall, Thomas the merchant wasn't quite able to hide his surprise at this newly built mansion.

"How should I say this... The count's taste is surprisingly subdued."

Nias agreed. "I like it—it's nice and functional. I was invited to an egg-shaped mansion once. It's hard to be at ease in a place that unusual."

It was the grand coming-of-age ceremony, and everyone Liam was acquainted with had been invited. It also served to show off his new residence now that it was completed, but those who had been invited found Liam's mansion rather modest. Not in scale, but in general appearance. It was certainly splendid, and many well-known artists had lent their talents to its creation, but in the Empire—where many nobles preferred novel designs—Liam's mansion was rather utilitarian. Sure, it was immense, but there were larger mansions, and its straightforward approach gave it a rather serene feel.

"It's just like the count to build something easy to live in like this. It's funny... He hasn't changed much despite the vast fortune he's acquired. I thought for sure he'd build this place out of gold!"

Thomas had been expecting Liam to tell him, "My mansion will be built entirely from gold, so I want all the gold ingots you can find!" However, it seemed that even Liam wouldn't take his love for gold that far.

"He did spend a good amount on it, but I'd say it was money well spent."

Eyeing the faces around them, Nias shrugged. "What a crowd, though. I guess the big merchants have all got their eye on him. There are people here from other weapons factories too."

Most of the guests were locals: government officials and soldiers of some standing in the domain. The rest mostly sought to do business on the planet, given its newfound success.

Thomas's shoulders sagged. "There aren't a lot of nobles, though. That's somewhat concerning."

Quite a few nobles from nearby territories had been invited, but many of them were absent.

Nias didn't think there wasn't much that could be done about that. "Well, I'm sure the neighboring nobles are a little uneasy about how he's suddenly gained so much power."

Rather than cooperate, many of the Empire's nobles actually fought with each other. *Some* were in attendance, however. These were failed nobles who didn't have the power to develop their territories and had come to try to ingratiate themselves with Liam, so that he would consider looking after them.

Thomas scanned these nobles' faces. "He's attracted plenty of poor nobles, though."

As for the reasons for their poverty, some had brought it on themselves, while others were genuinely deserving of pity. A number of them had formerly been vassals to House Banfield, and now that Liam had taken over the family and was reclaiming power, they hoped to be taken back under his protection. Their presence was a clear acknowledgment of Liam's power, but that didn't change the fact that they had come to take advantage of him.

Nias was rather indifferent to it all. "Well, the Empire can't take care of every little planet out in the boonies. The minor lords have no choice but to rely on the nobles with power."

While they were speaking, the ceremony commenced. The guests around them looked nervous. Liam must have arrived.

Thomas smiled. "He's actually a very affable person, but I suppose the rumors frighten people."

"I've always thought he was a good guy. He just bought a nice battleship from us recently too."

"You're a brave one, Miss Nias. I think Lord Liam allows you to get away with more than he would most people."

To be honest, I think these others are right to be afraid. That kind of power at his young age?

Despite having his territory and peerage forced upon him as a mere child, Liam had become a wise ruler. From the very beginning, he'd launched straight into heavy reforms. He tolerated no corruption in his court and had personally defended his people at the head of his army when raiders attacked. He was strict and severe, but a reliable lord to his subjects. He had invested most taxes back into the development of his territory, and the Empire valued him for properly paying his own taxes. On top of that, he had been regularly making payments on his family's astronomical debt.

Even if House Banfield's reputation had long ago become a poor one, Liam as an individual had slowly been building his own good reputation. There were officials and soldiers in his domain who would lay down their lives for him. The only things he had lacked were vassals and knights. But as Liam entered the chamber, a newly appointed knight walked at his side.

Thomas stroked his chin. "That would be Lady Christiana. I hear she's the first knight Lord Liam has taken into his service. She's said to be quite capable."

"Are you sure he didn't hire her just for her looks?"

"Well, I can't say that had nothing to do with it, but I've seen many knights, and she really is something special. You might say it's her aura; I'll bet she's a powerful one." Thomas then added, "I've heard rumors that she's the Princess Knight—the one from that nation that Goaz destroyed."

Nias was familiar. "The famous one? Isn't she the wrong age, though? The Princess Knight should be way older. She doesn't even look a hundred years old. That can't be right, can it?"

Thomas understood her doubts. "Well, they're just rumors. But if he really did have someone like that by his side, Lord Liam would truly have the makings of a wise ruler, the likes of which one seldom sees."

Had Liam heard all this, he would've been hopelessly confused. After all, he'd only worked this hard to develop his domain because if he didn't, he wouldn't have anything to squeeze from his subjects later. He had only cut down his corrupt officials because they'd personally pissed him off. He had only faced off against the pirates because he was assured to win. He was only paying his taxes and paying back his debt because it was beneficial to stay in the Empire's good graces. And he'd only hired Tia because of her good looks and loyalty, not because of comments he'd heard about her supposed rare skill. There hadn't been any sort of deeper reason for his actions. The man himself was under the impression that he was living selfishly as an evil lord.

The austere ceremony continued.

A tear spilled from Thomas's eye as he marveled at Liam's majestic appearance. "I wasn't wrong about Lord Liam. I'm so glad I stuck with him."

Nias agreed, though she thought the merchant's emotion was a bit much. "It's a relief for our factory to have a regular customer like him. I hope he keeps up the good work from now on. If he bought just a little more from us, I'd have no complaints at all."

Narrowing his eyes, Thomas warned her, "I think that'll be hard to achieve unless your factory makes further improvements to outward appearance and interior design. No matter how functional your ships are, if they're uncomfortable in form and operation, it's not going to win you any points."

Nias just pretended not to hear him.

One month after the ceremony, I was puzzling over a rather difficult dilemma.

"Would you say I'm living in luxury?"

It was Brian who responded to my question. "Hm? Well, I don't know much about other houses, but compared to our previous lords, I'd say you live rather frugally."

Seated at my desk with my chin propped up in my hands, I was starting to realize something.

I assumed I was living a life of luxury, but the money in

my accounts isn't going down at all. No matter how much I spend, it doesn't really make a dent.

"Frugally?"

"Yes, I believe so. Considering your position, I don't think there would be any harm in indulging yourself a little more."

Right. I mean, I am a count. But I don't know what level of "indulgence" befits a count.

I'd decided to hire musicians to play during my meals just to spend some of my money. It was something I figured rich people would have done in my earthly life. There was also loads of unused space in the huge mansion I'd built, which led me to consider what to do with it.

I could install a nice big pool to use whenever I want. No, I'll put a whole water park in here... Then I can have a wave pool, and a lazy river.

So I did, and the day it was completed, I amused myself by swimming backward in the lazy river.

And now my bath is a hot spring too! But I'm still living frugally? I really underestimated the standards in this world.

"What *is* luxury, Brian?"

"I'm not sure how to answer that, sir." Brian shot Amagi a silent plea for assistance, so she answered in his stead.

"According to my records, there was one count who turned an entire planet into a private resort, a sort of tourist retreat for him alone."

"What's the point of that?"

A tourist retreat for just one person? What use did it serve when he wasn't there? He could at least have let other people visit!

"If that is your reaction, you may simply not desire a great degree of luxury, Master," Amagi said. "Your seeking meaning in such things is the proof of the fundamental difference in your values. Luxury requires no such meaning; self-satisfaction is its only purpose. Considering your personality, perhaps it would be best for you not to strive for certain standards of luxury."

"Th-that's not true! I'm gonna live in luxury. I've got the money—I can do whatever I want with it!"

Brian studied me fondly. "Of course, sir. What would you like to do?"

My eyes darted about as I tried to come up with something. I'd already exhausted all my own ideas for indulgence. At the moment, no others occurred to me.

While I floundered, Amagi supplied a possibility. "Might I suggest a study abroad program?"

"Study abroad? I'm about to go for special training, aren't I? Isn't that already studying abroad?"

"I do not mean you, but your subjects. If your people learn the ways of the Capital Planet and in other territories, you will attain a populace with more varied views and knowledge. You could say this is a form of luxury, as it is not something you are required to do for your people."

Like, have people study abroad for fun? Is it luxury to use my money to make other people happy? It's true that I don't need my people to be well educated or anything; all they need to do is stay in line.

Brian seemed to agree with her. "I think that's a wonderful idea. You've mentioned before that since your territory has only recently been developed, your people still have much to learn in the ways of the arts and fashion. You could say that having them study abroad to acquire such nonessential knowledge is a form of luxury."

I recalled this past conversation Brian was referring to. "That's right! I know what they can learn abroad!"

The reason I still couldn't bring myself to pick up girls in my own domain was that persistent fashion problem. None of the girls here really did it for me. If people got out and saw more of the world, maybe things on that front would improve. At the very least, they should figure out that going to the beach in a wetsuit wasn't appealing. I'd never forget the day I found out it was considered fashionable here to stick a little umbrella on your head when you went out in the rain or bright sun. It had brought me to tears.

Art and fashion aren't things you need to learn in order to survive—people just trying to eke out a living can't afford to concentrate on such matters. I supposed it was a sort of luxury to be able to focus on them.

"Get things ready; I want to send as many people abroad as I can! We've got plenty of money to pay for it."

Amagi immediately began preparations. "I will formulate a plan of action and work it into your budget, Master. If we work quickly, we can collect applicants and begin sending them abroad next year."

"Nice. Now that's what I call luxury!"

Brian was dabbing the corners of his eyes, but I ignored him. "Sending your subjects abroad to study with your own money... It's just what I would expect of you, Master Liam."

I could barely understand what he was saying, his voice was so choked with sobs.

Anyway, I've just gotta make use of my money—as much as I can! I'm after luxury here. Evil lords must indulge themselves!

I'd gotten my hands on a vast fortune, so I wanted to spend it in whatever ways I could. I was on the right track to obtaining my ultimate goal.

One day, I'll be an evil lord who everyone will fear!

I'M THE **EVIL LORD** OF AN **INTERGALACTIC EMPIRE**

BONUS STORY Liam's Harem Plan

WHAT IS REQUIRED to be an evil lord? Money, violence...and women.

Since I'd obtained the alchemy box, a total cheat item, money was no longer a concern. I'd been able to pay off my debt without issue. That was one objective down.

As for violence: I'd acquired a most wonderful swordsmanship technique known as the Way of the Flash, and though I was sure I still had much to learn in that area, I figured I'd become a pretty decent knight at least. This meant I'd cleared my second objective as well.

"The only thing left is women!"

Thus, I prepared a room in my new mansion for this one. At a glance, it looked like an audience chamber a king might use in an RPG. I had set up a lavish throne for myself at the far end, and ridiculously ornate pillars supported the high ceiling, with a pool at the room's center. I'd created this ostentatious room while thinking *Evil lords are all about debauchery!* It was here that I planned on having beautiful women in swimsuits attend to me.

When it was ready, I invited Amagi and Brian inside to show off, but they didn't react very well to it.

"I see you have engaged in another of your silly little projects, Master."

"Master Liam, what do you intend to use this room for? I do not believe I heard anything about this project."

Well, I didn't think they'd respond well if I told them I wanted to make a harem chamber, so I kept it from them, but I'm not going to restrain myself! I'm an evil lord, after all.

"Why, this room exists to fulfill my dream."

Amagi tilted her head cutely. "Your dream?" she asked.

"That's right. This room exists to realize a dream I've long held. Have you heard the phrase 'conspicuous consumption'?"

Brian put a hand to his chin. "I believe I have."

"That's what I'm gonna do! I'll fill a whole pool with alcohol, hang meat from the pillars...conspicuous indulgences like that! Then I'll get a whole gaggle of girls and make a harem!" I spread my arms wide and gave a loud laugh, while Brian and Amagi looked on coldly.

Heh. I wouldn't expect these two to understand.

Amagi eventually moved her gaze from me to the empty pool. "Master, if you fill a pool with alcohol, it will evaporate, which is dangerous."

"Huh?"

"What purpose is there in filling the pool with alcohol in the first place? To drink it? It would be filthy."

I was a little flustered by Amagi's reasonable questions, but I'd put a good amount of thought into my plan.

"I-it's fine—the pool has a filter. And I don't think I'd drink that much of it anyway."

But now that I think about it, do I really want to drink alcohol people are swimming in? Uh, no. I'd rather have a normal drink than scoop something out of a pool.

"The mansion's filtration system would simply remove the alcohol and leave the pool filled with fresh water."

"Huh?"

Amagi's sound arguments kept on coming. "In the first place, what is the point of making a pool? If you would like to swim, it is safer to swim in water, and if you fill it with alcohol, it will just get filtered into water anyway. If you turned the filter off and left it as alcohol, it would not be healthy to swim in."

Having heard all of Amagi's points, Brian clenched his fist and said, "I must protest, Master Liam! And what do you mean by hanging meat from the pillars anyway?" So now it was Brian trying to rain on my parade.

"Wh-what's wrong with that? I can at least hang the meat, can't I?!"

"You cannot! What are you going to do with such unhygienic food, anyway? Eat it? If you want to eat meat, please only eat it once it's been properly stored and prepared!"

When I really stop to consider whether I'd want to eat meat that's just hanging around on the walls... Eh, I dunno if I would.

"Now that you mention it, maybe this is a little *too* conspicuous."

"You're exactly right. I urge you to reconsider these plans."

Then again, evil lords are supposed to be wasteful, aren't they? Even if there's no point to the trappings and they involve something unhealthy, I'm gonna make this a reality one way or another! Amagi and Brian may try to stop me, but I will *amass a harem in this chamber!*

"I'm not gonna give up on my dream of owning a harem, though! I am going to have women wait on me and entertain me in here!" My voice echoed through the huge room.

I'm sure these guys can't understand, but I won't back down on this one.

However, Amagi reacted unexpectedly to my passionate words. "I do not see an issue with that."

"What? You don't?" I thought they'd shoot down my plan for a harem right away too. They'd had so much to critique about the booze and the meat, but nothing about the harem? I eyed Amagi suspiciously, but she had all her usual composure.

"Is it really okay? All right, well, I'm gonna make one, then. The biggest harem there's ever been." I looked to see if she'd budge, but she showed no signs of speaking up.

On the other hand, Brian was getting worked up again. "You are the head of the family, Master Liam—a count, and the ruler of this planet. It is only natural for you to have a harem."

"O-oh?"

Brian started ranting, as if he were venting criticisms of me that had been building up in him. "Do you know how much I have worried about how modest you are, Master Liam? At first, I thought you were just too young to be interested in the opposite sex, but then you go and fall for honey traps left and right!"

Wait a second! When did I fall for a honey trap?

"Hey, I've never—"

"Have you forgotten Engineering Captain Nias, Master

Liam? You ordered an entire fleet from the Seventh Weapons Factory just to appease that one woman!"

Now that he mentions it, I have bought quite a lot from Nias. I just purchased that new flagship from her, in fact.

"Sure, sure, whatever. But I can really make a harem? 'Cause I will, you know!"

Brian looked incredulous. He leaned forward and began to lecture me. "Pardon my frankness, Master Liam, but you should already be involved with several women at this point. If something should happen to you, the family is done for. It might be a little early, but you must produce an heir."

All of a sudden, he's telling me to have a kid, but I just literally became an adult! In fact, I'm at an age in this world where some people are still treating me like a kid. It's way too soon for me to have a child of my own. Besides, I haven't even finished my education, so I'm not considered a full-blown noble yet either.

"That kind of came out of nowhere, don't you think?"

"It did not! You absolutely must produce an heir! If you take a formal wife, then the other potential heirs can form branch families. House Banfield doesn't have a single branch family!"

Well, there's plenty of things I'd like to say about this heir stuff, but it's true that House Banfield is in trouble without

any branch families. In game terms, it's like we've got zero lives banked, so if we die once, it's game over. I'm kinda surprised House Banfield lasted long enough for me to be born into.

"How is this my fault?"

"All I am saying is: it is your responsibility to provide the family with an heir as soon as possible!"

Lately, more and more people in my domain were using artificial insemination and even growing their babies in test tubes, but it was still deemed preferable for a mother to grow her baby in her own womb. I didn't know much about these topics beyond that. Did I really need to start thinking along these lines?

Amagi quickly got us back on track about the harem. "There is no problem with your having a harem, so please go ahead and indulge yourself to your heart's content."

"No problem, huh?"

"Correct. But as for 'conspicuous consumption,' there are many hygienic concerns."

"So that one's a no go."

I'd figured they would both be against the whole harem thing, but it truly looked like they were both in favor of it. I'd thought for sure they were going to say something like "You must not fall prey to lust!"

Well, if it's fine with them, then that cinches it. I'm gonna collect as many beautiful women as I can, and have all the fun I like as an evil lord!

"Well, let's get to it, then. Bring on the beauties! I'll start by carefully selecting each one myself..."

But just as I started fantasizing, Brian interrupted me. "Please wait, Master Liam."

"What is it? You were all for it a second ago, but now you're gonna complain?"

"No, I just wanted to ask exactly what scale you are envisioning for this harem."

Heh! I bet these two are thinking in realistic numbers, like ten women. That'd probably be considered large for a harem, right? But I'm an evil lord—I dream big! I mean, if I'm gonna exploit my subjects, I should have at least a hundred women.

"A hundred."

"One hundred!" Brian's eyes widened in surprise.

He's probably gonna tell me it'll be too much trouble to have that many, but I refuse to compromise on—

"Just one hundred?"

"Huh?"

Apparently, Brian had been surprised by something else.

"Will you really be satisfied with so few?"

"Uh, what? Isn't a hundred a lot? It's a lot, right, Amagi?"

In response, Amagi brought up several screens around me. They all showed profile pictures of women with short bios attached.

"I've taken the liberty of collecting some candidates myself. I have ten thousand here, and I was thinking that you could invite at least a thousand of them to live in the mansion."

"A thousand?!"

I was off by a whole digit? Do you really think I can handle that many women all on my own?

"Are you guys crazy? What would I do with that many?"

Trying to have a businesslike conversation about something so personal as the legion of women who'd be pleasuring me was becoming a little too embarrassing.

His expression grave, Brian tried to persuade me. "The number is not the issue. What is important is finding women who will please you. What matters is not the box, Master Liam, but its contents."

By "the box," I guess he means this chamber I've made. Instead of making a room to contain my harem, I should be collecting the contents of it first: the women.

"A thousand is too many, though!"

"None of this would be an issue if you invited women to the mansion yourself, Master Liam! For all your talk of a harem, you haven't chosen even a single woman to be beside you!"

"That's not true! I have Amagi, don't I?"

My butler cast a helpless look at Amagi, but even she seemed a little exasperated with me. "Master, I cannot bear your children."

"That's got nothing to do with it."

Brian covered his face and started to cry. "This simply will not do, Master Liam. If you would at least keep a few women you were fond of by your side, I would be able to rest easy."

"Shut up! You said it yourself: the number is not the issue! It's quality over quantity for me, and I'm not compromising on that!"

"Well, then I don't see your harem ever happening! Please, at least take this opportunity to meet *some* potential candidates."

Apparently there were plenty of oddball women who would easily volunteer if I said I wanted a concubine or mistress.

But that's not what I want! As an evil lord, I want to compel unwilling women to keep me company. Arata said that's what bad guys did in the dirty manga he read. What was the genre called? NTR? In my past life, my wife was stolen from me, but this time I want to be the

one doing the stealing! I can't just have women offering themselves to me.

"I want women with good looks and plenty of talent, but they can't just be subservient!"

Brian's expression finally turned to full-on despair. "What? You're the ruler of this planet, Master Liam; most women would do whatever you told them to!"

Amagi agreed with Brian. "You are very popular, Master."

Is every single person on this planet an idiot? Why the hell are they worshipping a villain like me? Well, jeez, that complicates things, doesn't it? I might not be able to find a single candidate for my harem on this planet.

"I can't choose them from my domain, then," I muttered, and Brian and Amagi both narrowed their eyes at me.

"I am beginning to doubt you're serious about creating a harem, Master Liam. To tell the truth, I am extremely worried."

Amagi added, "You have yet to make any sort of move on any of the mansion staff as well. I had expected you to pursue at least a few of them."

Why would I do that? I'm gonna customize my own harem. Like hell I'll just take somebody someone else has prepared for me! Come on, I'm an evil lord!

I'M THE **EVIL LORD** OF AN **INTERGALACTIC EMPIRE**

Afterword

HELLO, this is the author, Yomu Mishima.

What did you think of *I'm the Evil Lord of an Intergalactic Empire?!* A normal, decent person falls into the depths of despair in his earthly life, so he rethinks his destiny and decides to become a villain in his new life. This probably makes it sound like a serious story.

He ends up in an interstellar empire and struggles to adapt to the ways of this futuristic world. Although he aims to become an evil lord, he's instead treated as a wise ruler by all those around him. I would be delighted if you enjoyed Liam's unique struggle.

I hope readers of the original web novel liked the added scenes and such in this incarnation. I made a lot of improvements and revisions to this version, so the length has increased as well. Because of that, I perhaps don't have much room for an afterword, but anyway, I'm sure readers care more about the actual story than the author's afterword, so let's just call it the fruits of my labor, shall we?

Or would you have preferred an afterword from Brian? I couldn't quite figure out how to recreate that, so in the end, I just tossed the idea. Sorry to joke about stuff only the web readers will get!

Well, I hope we'll meet again in the next volume!

Congratulations!

I wonder if this world has plastic models?

高峰ナダレ
NADARE TAKAMINE